Branigan: Encouraged to Hope

The Barnabas Chronicles
Book 6

By

Ronna M. Bacon

Psalm 119:114 You are my hiding place and my shield; I hope in Your word. NKJV

Table of Contents

Chapter 1
Chapter 2
Chapter 3
Chapter 4
Chapter 5
Chapter 6
Chapter 7
Chapter 8
Chapter 9
Chapter 10
Chapter 11
Chapter 12
Chapter 13
Chapter 14
Chapter 15
Chapter 16
Chapter 17
Chapter 18
Chapter 19
Chapter 20
Chapter 21
Chapter 22
Chapter 23
Chapter 24
Chapter 25
Chapter 26
Chapter 27
Chapter 28
Chapter 29
Chapter 30
Chapter 31

Chapter 32
Chapter 33
Chapter 34
Chapter 35
Chapter 36
Chapter 37
Chapter 38
Chapter 39
Chapter 40
Chapter 41
Epilogue
Dear Readers

Reaching into the backseat of the small SUV he preferred to drive, Branigan Clery caught the handle of his briefcase, and then paused, his hand on the car door, looking around the small building lot that he had parked in. He shook his head. Why me, Lord? Are there not others who could have been called in to set up the security system for this small trucking company? A brand new building and likely not wired for this. I know, Lord, I know. It's my calling first and foremost, but just for once I would love an easy job. Something tells me this one is going to try my patience well past what I can handle right now. Having my friends go through what they did has worn us all out. None of us were prepared for any of it.

Closing the car door, he paced through the gravel parking lot, to stand for a moment staring at the small office building and then stepping back to stare at the larger building, the garage for the company, to hold the mechanics shop and warehouse. He wondered at the two buildings and then shrugged. It didn't matter to him, or at least, it shouldn't. He reached for the door and walked through, the green steel door with a window closing quietly behind him. He frowned. Nothing to indicate he had entered.

He stood for a moment at the reception counter before placing his briefcase on it and then wandering around the small waiting room, studying the windows and then the door, looking at it from a security standpoint. He nodded to himself, pleased with what he saw. Someone had done their homework, he thought.

He spun as he heard footsteps behind him, his heart pounding for a moment. He was jumpy, he admitted, and prayed for that to leave. It wouldn't do to show that, not when he was here to set up a security system. His employer, Barnabas Carey, of the Barnabas Foundation, had asked him to. The client was a board member of the Foundation and also a fellow church member, although Branigan had to admit he didn't know him that well.

"Branigan. Thanks for coming. It's going to be good to get the security set up. I've been on edge ever since we moved out to this location." Brett Danby grinned as he extended his hand for Branigan to shake. "I know. I know. I should have had you involved from the beginning, but you were helping out your friends, and I didn't want to intrude."

"Brett. It would not have been an intrusion. I don't think this will take that many days. I'll need to go over your buildings and then sit down with you to have a chat about what you want. By the way, I didn't hear any chime to let you know I had arrived."

Brett grinned. "No, you wouldn't. Guenivere has trouble with chimes, always has had for some reason. So the electrician wired up a light for us that indicates when someone enters. I would like to keep that but connect it to a video feed if we can. A monitor set up in my office and in the break room, as well as in the warehouse would suit me just fine."

"Shouldn't be a problem." Branigan reached for his briefcase. "Let's start with a tour. I didn't realize you had moved out this far."

"We needed the extra room, now that the business has grown. Guenivere has some ideas that she wants to try, and I must say, she is usually right with her thoughts."

Branigan finally settled down in the office Brett had taken him to, his notes spread out around him, his computer open to the program he used to plan his projects. He heard movement out in the hallway as well as quiet conversation. He tilted his head. That must be Guenivere, he thought. He didn't think that she had been around much, he hadn't noticed her at church. Soon, lost in his thoughts, he ignored the activity outside the office.

A loud, coarse laugh brought his head up, and his dark gray eyes narrowed. That was not Brett, he thought. He rose and quietly moved to stand in the hallway, his eyes searching for the commotion, and commotion it was. He could hear a young woman's voice raised in protest and he walked forward, his very stance stating he would not tolerate any nonsense towards her.

Guenivere Danby faced the man standing across the counter from her, her curiously coloured aqua eyes holding the fright she was trying to tamp down, without much success, she thought. Her father had had to leave, and she felt all alone, forgetting the younger man her father had said was working in the extra office.

"No, you can't tour the warehouse. Only employees do." She straightened up as tall as she could, trying to bluff him.

He laughed again. "Oh, but I can. And you are going to show me. I intend to become a partner of your father's. We'll play nice, won't we?" He reached for her hand, his eyes suddenly rising to stare behind her.

Guenivere gave a muffled shriek as arms encircled her and pulled her back against a tall strong body.

"Guenivere, hon. Do you need some help out here? I'm sorry I didn't hear the door. I was involved in that task for your Dad." Branigan did not hesitate to intrude.

"I can use some help. This gentleman was on his way out. Only he can't seem to find the door." Her hands had risen to grip Branigan's, and he wondered at the tightness of her hold.

His head tilted slightly so he could watch her face before one hand came up to tuck the long blond hair behind one ear. Then he glanced over at the man standing there, hatred and evil emanating from him. He frowned once more. What is this all about, Lord? You knew I was needed here today.

Branigan walked around Guenivere and tucked her behind him. In a low voice, he muttered, "If I say run, run to somewhere you can lock yourself away. Don't even question me." He felt her head nodding against his back and bit back a grin. She had buried her face against him.

—

"Now, you sir. The door is behind you. I would suggest you leave and don't return."

The man sneered. "I don't think so. You can't tell me what to do."

Branigan moved suddenly, around the counter and with the man's arm twisted behind his back, before anyone could realize what he was doing.

"I do believe you were asked to leave. Let me escort you to your vehicle. If you do not leave, we will certainly call for the authorities to come on out and escort you to their building for a tour there. Somehow, I don't think you'll like that tour."

Branigan shoved the man forward, directly to his car, wrenching open the door and shoving him into it.

"Now, sir, you will leave. You will not return. If you do, they will call for help."

Slamming his door shut, a look of hatred still aimed at Branigan, the man sped away. Branigan watched for a moment before he heard a soft voice from beside him.

"He's gone?" Guenivere had appeared, not content to wait in the office.

"He has, and you should not be out here." Branigan stared at her in disbelief.

Guenivere stared up at him, her eyes narrowing as she took in the dark brown hair and gray eyes. Lord, he looks just like the image Mom always wove into my bedtime stories. I can't do this right now. Or at least I don't think I can.

"I know, but I was afraid he would hurt you."

Branigan swung her around, his hand to her lower back to direct her back into the office. "He wouldn't have. Not in the open like this. He's a bully and they work best from undercover." His head tilted as he heard a sound and then he was shoving Guenivere towards the building. "Run, Guenivere. Run."

She took off, fright welling up as she heard the sound of a racing motor. She prayed for that they would make it in time. She heard the sound of gravel spraying as the car raced back into the lot and then slowed somewhat. The next sound she heard was the sickening sound of a body hit by the car and then landing on the ground. She stopped suddenly and spun, hands to her mouth as she saw Branigan sprawled on the ground, the car near him, and the man who had accosted her standing with his arm leaning on the open door.

His eyes raised to hers and he smirked an evil grin at her. "Next time, it will be you. I'll be in touch. I will be a part owner of this company. Just you wait."

She stared in horror as the gravel sprayed from his tires as he took off before she was running towards Branigan, to drop to her knees, a hand to his chest as he sprawled on his back. Tears gathered in her eyes, and she angrily brushed at them. This is no time to cry, girl. He needs help, only I don't want to leave him. She heard her name called and looked up to see the mechanic racing towards her.

"Douglas, we need an ambulance and the police. Branigan was just run down."

Douglas nodded. "I called. They're on their way. What was his problem?"

"I don't know for sure." She stared down at Branigan. "He made him leave but he came back. Dad wasn't here." She looked up, such fright in her eyes that Douglas drew in a breath. "What would have happened if Branigan hadn't have been?"

Douglas dropped down beside her. "God had you, Guenivere. That He did. Run and get a blanket for me. We'll try and keep him comfortable."

She ran, flinging open the door and racing for the break room, reaching for the blanket her mother had left there before she turned. Something was off in there, she thought, and shrugged, her thoughts going back to the man laying out in their parking lot, unconscious and all because of her.

Chapter 2

Running back through the building, Guenivere tripped over a package dropped near the door, landing on her hands and knees, shock and pain hitting her before she was on her feet again, the blanket in her arms, heading for Branigan.

Douglas looked up as she approached, standing for a moment, his hand out to stop her before he reached for the blanket, to shake it out and cover Branigan.

"Douglas? Has he been awake?" Guenivere stared up at him with hope in her eyes, that died away when he shook his head. She was on her knees, Branigan's wrist in her hand as she felt for a pulse. "It's weak, Douglas. Where are they?"

"They are their way." He could faintly hear the sounds of the sirens approaching. "I can hear them."

She nodded, her hand out to touch Branigan's face, trying to brush away the small bits of debris that's covered one cheek. "Why? All he had to do was leave and not come back."

"What did he want?" Douglas paced. "We've never had any trouble. Not like this."

Guenivere looked up, shaking her head. "I don't really know. He never said." She turned as she heard a heavy motor and the paramedic rig appeared behind the police cruiser that slid to a stop near the building.

She didn't let go on Branigan's hand, feeling that she had to hold on to it, that for some reason he needed her to. She just knew he was going to affect her life and that she didn't understand or really know if she wanted that.

Alice stood for a moment, studying the three, before she approached, her breath indrawn for a moment as she recognized Branigan.

"What happened?" Alice stared between Douglas and Guenivere, waiting for one of them to speak. "I asked, what happened?"

Douglas drew Guenivere to her feet and away from Branigan, almost fighting to do so. He frowned. This was not the young lady he had watched grow from a toddler. He was a long-time friend of her father's.

"I'm not sure, Alice. I was working away and heard the commotion out here. By the time I got to here, he was on the ground and Guenivere beside him on her knees."

Guenivere nodded, and then shuddered. "He was here again. I've seen him lurking around. But he has never come into the building. Why would he want a tour? Why would he say he was going to be a partner with Dad? That won't happen."

Alice's pen paused above her notepad, as she studied the younger woman. "He said that. Walk me through from the beginning. Then, I'll have to have you come in and give a formal statement."

Guenivere talked, giving what information she could, her eyes not leaving Branigan. The paramedics had hesitated for a few seconds as they recognized him, before they were down beside him, assessing him, reaching for a neck collar and backboard before shifting him to a stretcher and then heading for the rig. Guenivere broke away from Alice and ran after them.

"Please, let me go with him? He was hurt saving me." She didn't give them a chance to respond before she hopped up into the rig and huddled into a corner, the two men exchanging glances and a shrug.

Branigan stirred for a moment, his eyes flickering open and closed, a groan rising from him as the pain hit. He only had one thought. Guenivere. Was she safe?

"Guenivere?" His voice was rough with pain. "Is she okay?"

Pat, the paramedic riding in the back, shook his head, his eyes on Guenivere.

"She's fine, buddy. She's right here."

"She is? Where?" Branigan tried to rise, the straps around him keeping him flat on his back. "What are these? I need to get up and find her."

Guenivere had slid closer, Pat's finger beckoning to her, before her hand touched Branigan's face.

"I'm here. Right here."

"You are?" Branigan blinked as he tried to twist to see her. "You're okay? He didn't hurt you?"

"No, you made me run. Now, lie still. We don't know how hurt you are."

Branigan's hand found hers, the clasp tight enough that she couldn't remove her hand. She stared at Pat, who shook his head as he bit back a snicker. Lady, he just claimed you, whether you realize it or not. This is not what Branigan does.

Guenivere felt the rig backing up the hospital entrance and she ducked her head to look out the back door before she turned back to Branigan. He had not let go of her hand, no matter how she had twisted hers. Pat had just shaken his head.

"He's not letting go, you do know that?" He grinned at the look she threw him. "I don't think he'll let go even when we lower the stretcher. So, here's what we do. If you can stand up a bit and walk down the rig, once we get to the point we're lowering the legs, we'll lift you down. You can stay with him for now."

Guenivere nodded, a sudden fear in her heart. What if he didn't recover? What if he was really hurt? How would she ever live with herself? She followed Pat's instructions, not seeing the amused look shared between the two paramedics, once more trying to release her hand.

Doc Andrews, friend to all the men who were employed by Barnabas Foundation and father figure to them, watched, a frown on his face before he saw Pat shaking his head. He'd find out what was going on with Branigan. This was not him, Doc knew, and then had a sudden sense that Branigan too had found his lady in the midst of an adventure as the younger men liked to say.

He reached for his stethoscope as he listened to Pat's report, quiet words spoken among them. Doc turned, reaching for the requisitions needs to order bloodwork, imaging studies, as he kept turning to watch Guenivere. She stood, her hand still tight in Branigan's, her other hand lightly touching his hair, not aware of how disheveled she looked.

"Guenivere?" Doc finally stood beside her, a light of amusement showing in his eyes. "How well do you know Branigan?"

Her head flipped around, her mouth rounded in surprise and her eyes huge.

"I don't. I didn't meet him until today when he stepped in to help me. Dad had him out at the buildings to see about a security system." Her face darkened. "Now, look at him."

"We know, Guenivere. I just wondered seeing as he won't let go of you. Pat said you both tried."

"We did." Guenivere looked back at Branigan, not realizing her face had softened.

Doc nodded. Another one, Lord. What will these two go through?

Chapter 3

Doc had finally managed to loosen Branigan's hand enough that Guenivere could pull her free, and she rubbed at it as she paced the waiting room. She had had to leave, much against her wishes, as he was further assessed.

Hearing her name, she spun, catching her balance with a hand against the nearby wall. Her father was walking towards her, accompanied by Alice, and then she frowned. The man who had accosted her and then run down Branigan was standing in the doorway, a smirk on his face. She grew angry and then stomped towards him, Alice spinning before she followed behind her.

"Why are you here? You're not wanted here or on our property."

"Too bad, little lady. Get used to me being around." He took a look past her at Alice heading his way, her hand resting on the weapon on her belt, before he looked down at Guenivere with a sneer. "I'm gone. We'll talk again, little lady. A nice quiet dinner, just you and me." He spun and was gone, Alice on his heels, her hand catching his arm and stopping him.

Brett stood with his arm around a now-trembling Guenivere.

"Lass? Who was that?"

Guenivere struggled to speak, tears of fear choking her. "That's him, Dad. He's the one who said he would be your partner." She looked up at her father. "Do you know him?"

Brett shook his head. "No, I don't. And you know I don't plan on taking on a partner. "I'm sorry, Guenivere. I would not have left had I known."

"But you had to. You had no choice. You left Branigan with me." She spun, heading back for the exam rooms, as her father caught her arm and stopped her. "Dad?" She turned her head, a frown in place.

"You can't go back there, lass. Not yet. You're not next of kin, no matter how tightly he held your hand." He grinned at his daughter, looking young and carefree for a moment. "I hear tell he claimed you."

"He did what?" Guenivere's voice rose as she finished. "No, he didn't." Her head was shaking in the negative as she stared at her father. "No, he didn't, Dad. He couldn't have." When her father didn't respond, she sighed. "Pat muttered something along those lines. I don't see it."

Brett's arm came around his daughter as he drew her to seats where they could see the doors, his heart and mind in a turmoil as he prayed, trying to find the words he needed. Lena, you need to be here. You should be the one explaining this, but God seems to think I should be.

"Dad?" Guenivere's voice held a tone he had not heard before, a mixture of despair, hope, longing and denial..

Brett sighed. "I know of Branigan just from being around Barnabas. He has a good heart, lass. He has never dated, has never shown interest in any lady. Not until today. Whether it was because you were in danger or not, I would have to ask him that. But don't block his friendship from your heart. Pray that God will show you His will. I see the spark of interest you have. You are a beautiful, compassionate Godly young woman. I have seen the interest in the young men who cross your path, but you haven't shown any interest in anyone. Not until today"

She leaned her head on her father's shoulder. "I know, Dad. I didn't want to put out false hope or ruin a friendship. I just never felt God was leading that way with any of them." She looked down at the hands she was rubbing together. "I don't know what it was about Branigan. He just appeared behind me, called me hon, and then shoved me behind him to protect me." She paused, at a loss for words. "He made me feel safe and cherished at the same time. Does that make sense?"

"Perfect sense, Guenivere. It's what you've been raised with." Her mother's arm came around her.

"Mom? You're here? You're supposed to be in school, teaching!" Guenivere stared at her mother, dismay on her face.

"You needed me. Will Peters stopped by and asked me to come." She grinned, looking so much like her daughter.

"He did? Then, I guess it's okay." She looked past her mother as she heard footsteps and then was on her feet, almost running for Doc as he approached.

Barnabas Carey stood for a moment, assessing the situation, seeing Doc's nod at him. Breck, who worked directly with him, as his second in command, stood beside him, a small grin on his face.

"I didn't see that coming, did you?"

"What coming?" Barnabas had a good idea where Breck was heading with his words, but hid his grin.

"Branigan and Guenivere. I wouldn't have put those two together."

"Danger does that. We know that from the other five who went through their adventures, shall we say?" Barnabas paused, his mind racing. "But, yeah, I can see it. Guenivere seems quiet but she has a side to her that she doesn't show many. Branigan would bring it out. And she would bring the stability he needs."

"That she would." Breck watched as Doc led Guenivere away before he headed for Brett, greeting the older couple. "Any word?"

"Not to us. Now, to our daughter, I would say that there has been." Brett grinned. "I hear tell Branigan claimed her."

Barnabas grinned. "That's what Will said when he called. I'll head back in a bit, talk to Doc, see what paperwork I need to sign as his next of kin." He leaned back against the wall. He felt old, worn out and tired. He knew why. It always hit him about this time of year, and he refused to admit it or talk to anyone.

Chapter 4

His head tossing restlessly, Branigan fought against the nausea that welled in his stomach, not sure why he felt like he did. His hand reached for the sore spot in his head, before a hand gently lowered it back to his chest. His hand flipped to grasp that hand. A lady's hand, he thought. It wouldn't be one of my friend's ladies. It's a left hand and has no rings on it.

Guenivere watched with concern as Branigan moved restlessly. It was her fault, she thought, that he was in this situation. She didn't like it. Alice and Will had been around, assuring her that the man who had accosted her was in jail, and would be for a while. He had a number of police departments very anxious to speak with him.

The door opened quietly and Guenivere had footsteps approaching her. She tried not to let her sudden fear overwhelm but found it difficult. She looked up at the man, just older than her, she thought, who had stopped at the other side of the bed, his eyes on Branigan before he looked up. A grin crossed his face.

"And you are Guenivere? I have seen you around town and church, but have never had the pleasure of meeting you. Not until Branigan claimed you." His grin widened as her eyes narrowed and her mouth opened and closed. "I'm Baird, a good friend of Branigan. Thank you for what you did."

"For what I did? I didn't do anything. He's the one who got hurt, saving me." She blinked rapidly for a moment, before she looked back up at him. "I've seen you at church. With your wife and it is her brother?"

"Berneen and Darby. Yes. She has commented in the past she would like to get to know you, but you have disappeared so quickly."

Guenivere nodded. "I have. I don't always do well with crowds and then too I volunteer in a small chapel outside of town."

"I have heard that." Baird studied her, seeing the strain she had been under, but also steel that had been tried and strengthened running through her. "Has he been awake?'

"Not really. Just rousing a bit." She felt a tug on her hand and looked down, to find Branigan watching her, his eyes clear. "Branigan? You're awake. Your friend is here so I can leave."

Branigan's hand tightened even more on hers. "No, I need you to stay. Please?" His head turned slightly at the snicker Baird couldn't contain. He frowned, bringing on a headache. "Baird? Why did you make me go and do that? What are you doing here?" He craned his neck to look around him. "Berneen?"

"She's in the waiting room, didn't want to disturb you. Besides we were told only two visitors and you already have one." He smirked again at Guenivere as she gasped at his audacity.

"Give it a rest. Help me up. I need to get out of here." He raised his head and then let it flop back on the pillow, his eyes closing against the pain, not seeing the look of horror and concern that flooded Guenivere's face.

"Branigan, you need to lie still. That's what you were told."

"I don't remember. I want to go home. I hate hospitals." His eyes closed and he slept again, pain flickering across his face.

"Guenivere?" When she looked up at him, Baird smiled. "Now, are you okay? I heard you had quite the time today."

"I did." She frowned. "Why go after us? That I don't understand." She sighed. "If Dad had not asked Branigan to take a look at our security, he wouldn't be in this hospital bed right now."

"On the contrary, he is glad to be there, knowing he saved you. Have you even considered what might have happened to you, had he not been there?" Baird tamped down his frustration and, yes, anger as Guenivere stared at him, a blank look on his face. "Guenivere. I've talked to Alice. That man, the one who appeared in your office? He's wanted by many forces, for kidnapping, assault and murder. He would have taken you, hid you somewhere, and then used you against your Dad."

Guenivere was horrified. Her hand covered her mouth as she fought against her emotions. "That can't be true!" At Brady's nod, she looked up, her eyes clouded with tears of fear and anger. "He would have, wouldn't he? He was reaching for me when Branigan spoke up. How do I repay him?"

"He won't want that, Guenivere. All he wants is to know you are safe." Baird stared down at his friend for a moment, his thoughts muddled as he tried to sort through them. "He has staked a claim to you, whether you accept it or not. He will not walk away from you." He looked up to see her shaking her head. "I repeat, he will not walk away from you. For now, consider that you two are a couple, and that you have a boyfriend. That's how he'll want to play it out. For his sake and for yours, as well as your parents', think about it. With Branigan, you have the backing of us all from the Foundation."

"And there are so many of you." Guenivere paused. "What did he mean, when he said something to Dad about being paid by the Foundation? Doesn't he work for a company?"

"He doesn't. He works for Barnabas, who sources out the companies, businesses and individuals that needs security set up." Baird paused, trying to think of how to phrase what he needed to say. "For us all, we are paid through the Foundation. We are hired on as employees by businesses and companies, but they don't pay us. That way, they are free to hire someone else without worrying where the money needs to come from. That's how the Foundation was set up. Barnabas and his father wanted to encourage others, just like Barnabas in the Bible. I'm sorry. I've startled you with that." He looked back down at Branigan before looking up. "I think that should have been a conversation you had with our friend."

"No, it's okay. This isn't going to go anywhere." She gently extricated her hand, laying it for a moment against Branigan's cheek, feeling the end-of-day stubble there, before she walked away without another word, the door swishing closed behind her

Baird watched her walk away, before he turned back to his friend, a prayer for healing rising in his heart. Branigan, she's your heart. You show that by your actions. Please, dear Lord? Help them. Keep them safe. I don't want them to go through what five of us have, but I fear that is exactly what will happen.

Chapter 5

Glaring at first Brady and then Brennen, Branigan slumped back onto the hospital bed. It was two days later, and he was fighting to be released, wanting to be home, but wanting to be with Guenivere. That didn't make sense to him, but the other men had laughed when he had asked where she was and if she was okay. He really couldn't remember much of what had happened since the early morning of the day he had been run down.

"Take it easy, Branigan. The physician said you could be released. We're just waiting for your paperwork." Brady and Brennen exchanged glances, knowing that Branigan would want to head to only one place and that would be where he could find Guenivere.

"I need out of here. I left all my work at the trucking company. They need that security set up yesterday." He stood, a hand on the bed rail to balance himself before he turned to his friends. "Either you help me or I walk out of here on my own. Doc said he'd see me at home but I can't go there. Not yet."

"We know that, Branigan. Give us a few minutes to round up your paperwork and then we'll take you to your lady." Brennen smirked at the glare sent his way before he turned as the door opened.

Guenivere stood for a moment, her eyes on the three men before she headed for Branigan, a sheaf of paperwork in her hand.

"Branigan? What are you doing?"

He paused, taking in her beauty, before he grinned. "Looking for you, I think." He ignored the smothered laughter that sounded. "Forget these two jokers. Can you spring me?"

Hiding her own smile but her eyes brimming with laughter and mischief, Guenivere tapped at her chin before she nodded. "I can. I have your paperwork right here. Mom said that seeing as you were hurt on our property, you are to come and stay with us for the next week. And yes, Doc has agreed to that. In fact, he encouraged it." She frowned as she recalled the eagerness with which Doc had responded to her question. "And yes, all of your friends are welcome to come and visit. The more the merrier, Mom said, although she will limit them if there are too many, just for the first two days."

Brady and Brennen had been listening with interest to the conversation before they exchanged a glance, seeing Branigan had given in and was waiting as he saw the nurse approaching with the wheelchair. This was unusual for him. He was usually the one who was stubborn and ready to head into a fight, not sitting back and letting himself heal.

Watching as Guenivere drove carefully away, Brennen's head turned as he heard footsteps stop beside him. Barnabas stood there as did Buckley, their friend and minister.

"I thought you were bringing Branigan back to the building." Barnabas was puzzled.

"That was the plan. Doc had other ideas, it would seem. I gather he talked to Lena Danby and Branigan has been taken in there for the week. Guenivere stated it was because he was hurt on their property, but I think there's more."

"She feels responsible for him being hurt, seeing as he was trying to protect her." Buckley just shook his head. "Are we allowed to visit or are we banned from the house?"

"Guenivere has graciously told us we can visit but we have to limit the number at a time." Brennen shook his head as he remembered the feisty, determined look on her face. "I wouldn't want to cross her."

Barnabas looked surprised. "I wouldn't have thought that."

"They're a couple, Barnabas, whether they acknowledge it or not. They will do what they can to protect one another. It's up to us to back them and help." Brady walked away, leaving the others staring after him before staring at one another.

"He's right. That's what he did with Fynn." Brennen looked around, and then spoke. "I saw the two together. It's not something I've seen, not even with the other five. There's a spark there that didn't come from the problem the other day."

"No, Branigan has been searching, I know, for the helpmeet God planned for him." Barnabas halted his words, not wanting to destroy a confidence from Branigan.

"I think we all are, Barnabas." Brennen walked away as well, heading after Brady, to catch a ride home with him.

Buckley snickered, drawing Barnabas' eyes to his face before Barnabas laughed as well.

"I guess we got told." Buckley laughed out loud. "And he's right."

"I know he is. It doesn't make it any easier if the rest of us have to face what they did." Barnabas pulled out his keys. "Let's go. No use us hanging around here when they've already left."

"I'll stop in later to see how he's doing." Buckley paused, his eyes raised, searching. He could feel eyes on them, but why? Branigan was not there.

Guenivere stood for a moment, a few hours later, in the doorway to her parents' living room, her eyes on Branigan as he lay, stretched out on the couch, seemingly asleep, one arm flung over his eyes. She knew he was hurting, but didn't know how to make it better for him. That she couldn't do. Only God would heal him.

She felt hope rising within her. Hope that what had terrified her, terrorized her and suppressed her would be over. God, is Branigan the one to help with that? I need hope, to feel that I can finally live as I should, for You, for myself.

Branigan stirred as he felt her hand on his forehead, his hand reaching for hers, and pulling her down to sit beside him as he sat up. His free hand rubbed at his temple for a moment as he watched her and the emotions flickering across her face. She's hurting a lot harder than just from this. How do I help her?

"Guenivere? Want to talk?"

She shrugged, her eyes on his face. "I'm not sure. How are you feeling?" She chose a safe topic of conversation or so she hoped.

He grinned, knowing she was deflecting his question. "Better. The headache is there but not as bad. I know I am battered and bruised. The gravel did a number on me even through my clothing. The shower helped. But that's not what I asked."

She looked down at their hands, not even trying to pull hers free. She had given up on that, realizing that Branigan would not let go of it unless he wanted to, and it certainly didn't appear as if he did.

"I know. I just don't know how to express what I need to say." She looked up, longing in her eyes to do just that. "You are the first one who has ever asked me that, in the way you meant. You're digging deep."

He nodded. "I know I am. I have to. I lost my parents to a hit and run accident. They were gone before I could even say goodbye. I was only twelve, with no siblings and no other relatives. Being raised in foster care isn't always the easiest or the best. I had good foster parents, who raised me to continue to believe and trust in God. They asked the hard questions, waited, and then asked again until I was ready to talk. It helped. I want the same for you. It will free you to be who God meant you to be."

She felt hope rising within her once more, hope that she had not felt for years. She hadn't been able to talk to her parents, to tell them of the threat that she had encountered when she was a young teenager. It had reflected on her life and in a negative way, she realized, not letting her live her life as she should have.

Chapter 6

Branigan paused in the garden area of the Danby yard early the next morning. He had not slept all that well, his mind not wanting to shut down and let him. He was worried about Guenivere, more worried than he wanted to admit. He felt that what had happened, the man who had appeared, was not working on his own. He couldn't use a computer, Doc had warned him not to, and he needed to. He had research to do. Branigan sighed. This is not how he had planned to spend the weekend, he thought. He had had plans to go away on the Friday night and come back early on the Monday morning, to find a little cabin he could hide in. He was tired.   Having gone through their adventures with his five friends, he wasn't willing or ready to face it himself.

Turning as he heard footsteps approaching, Brannigan reached for the mug of coffee handed to him. Brett watched him closely, mindful of what Doc had said.

"Branigan, I or rather we will never be able to thank you for what you did yesterday." His hand went up at Branigan's protest. "I know, Branigan. You did what you feel anyone would have done. It scared me when Guenivere told me what had happened. She's fearless to a point, but there is a depth to her where she keeps things hidden that she never shows to anyone. I know there was something in the past that has affected her. She has never said. I have asked her friends and they either don't know or won't say, not wanting to break a confidence."

Branigan nodded, sitting in one of the deck chairs on the back patio, his mug of coffee going onto the table beside it. He didn't know quite how to approach Brett.

"Brett? What happened all those years ago? It has to have been when she was young."

Brett nodded. "Something did and we have no idea what. We've watched her. Been careful with her. She won't let us smother her." He pointed a finger at Branigan even as he grinned. "You holding her hand? That's unusual. She usually shuns any contact with the young men of her acquaintance, content just to be part of a group. For her to give in and let you? That tells me you have made a connection with her that others haven't."

Branigan nodded. "I guess. I'm not like that. I don't push. I haven't been dating." He sat back, reaching for the mug of coffee to sip at it, the early morning nature sounds ringing in his ears. He hesitated before speaking, not quite sure how to word what he needed to say. "You have a beautiful, caring, compassionate daughter, Brett. I would like to spend time with her, to get to know her. Her friendship is one I treasure already." He looked over at the older man, finding him studying him closely. "I have no idea where this will go or how your daughter feels."

Brett nodded, confident that Branigan had showed his heart. His head bowed and an audible prayer rose. Branigan stared at him for a moment before his own eyes closed.

"Branigan, all I can say is watch her heart and yours. If you don't believe this will go anywhere, then stop where you are right now." Brett rose, his eyes in the distance, hearing the sounds of a neighbour's car door closing before it drove away. The normal everyday sounds of his neighbourhood. He looked back down at Branigan. "But somehow, some way, Lena and I believe that you have been brought into Guenivere's life and that you will be the one to help her." He walked away, heading back into the house, leaving the younger man staring after him before Branigan's eyes closed and he prayed.

Guenivere stood for a moment, eyes closed, breathing in the scents from the last summer roses near the house. She slipped silently into the chair her father had vacated, her eyes on Branigan as he prayed, knowing that somehow he was praying for her.

Branigan stirred finally, feeling refreshed in his heart and soul, knowing that he had lifted up his burdens and hopes and dreams and that God heard and understood. If Guenivere was the one for him, God would lead. If not, he had asked that their hearts be protected.

"Hi!"

His head whipped around and he closed his eyes for a moment as the headache pounded behind his eyes. He squinted, seeing Guenivere with her hands to her mouth, a look of horror on her face.

"I'm sorry. I didn't mean you to do that."

He reached for her hand, fascinated with the neatness of the nails and the slenderness of her fingers. "It's not your fault. I forgot and moved too quickly." He grinned suddenly. "So, what are we up to today? Do you go into work? And can I come?"

She stared at him for a moment before her mouth snapped closed. "No, I'm not working today. Dad wants me to work from home for the next couple of days. He has your plans for the security system and Barnabas called in a friend of Fynn's, I think he said, to help."

"Joseph. Yes, he's a friend of Fynn. Do you know her?"

Guenivere shook her head. "No, I can't say that I have met the ladies from the Foundation." She sighed, knowing she would be bearing her heart to him with her next words. "I would like to get to know her and the others. I have a couple of friends but they are more interested in things that don't interest me. I'm not one for dating anyone and everyone. I don't like movies. I don't travel well." She looked up at his snicker and then glared at him. "What did I say that was so funny?"

"You could be describing me to some extent. Since I moved her from PEI, I have pretty much stayed in the area. The guys and I have travelled some. I had planned on heading up north just a bit, up the peninsula to a small cabin this weekend, just to get away. I'm sure you are aware of what has transpired with five of my friends."

She leaned forward, her eyes intent on him. "That. That's what I don't get. Why did God let them go through that?"

Branigan shrugged. "I don't really understand it myself but each of the couples said they had to, to resolve past issues, to find the ones responsible for evil, to begin to become the people God meant them to be." He hesitated, not sure how to express himself. "I'm not sure I'm saying it right."

"You are. God allowed what happened to bring them into a closer walk with Him and to use them in ways we don't understand."

Branigan nodded. "That's it. Exactly. What I was trying to say." He groaned. "No, that's not how I wanted to word that." He looked at her, his face straight but mischief gleaming in his eyes. "I lose my train of thoughts and can't put a sentence together when I'm around you."

Guenivere's head whipped up and she stared at him, her mouth open until he gently tapped under her chin, causing it to close.

"I've surprised you, I see." He reached for one of her hand, finding her fingers curling around his. "I want to date you, Guenivere. Explore our friendship. I know from your Dad that you don't date. Nor do I."

She sighed. "Dad's been talking." When he shook his head, she frowned. "He must of. There's no way you would ask this on your own."

"Who did this to you, Guenivere? Who beat you down so you don't even recognize your own beauty and worth. Yes, your Dad mentioned that you kept to home, didn't seem to be interested in the men of your acquaintance, but he did not, and I repeat, he did not ask me to date you. I had that idea all on my own. I did ask his approval, if you want to call it that."

Hope began to rise in Guenivere's heart. Was he the one, Lord? Would he be the one she could trust enough to help her find the teen who was now a man somewhere in the area who had beaten her down in her spirit all those years ago, made her feel ugly to the core, even though she wasn't? And just why had she let him?

"Branigan? You do need to rest." She sat back, her eyes watchful. "And yes, I would like to go out with you." Her hand raised as his mouth opened to speak, a light in his eyes that startled her. "First, you heal. Then we talk."

Chapter 7

Hearing his name called, Barnabas paused in his walk through town and turned. Breck was running towards him.

"Breck? I thought you had to be in court for that case this morning."

"He took a plea deal just as the court was about to begin." Breck pointed towards a local cafe. "Do you have time for coffee? We need to talk."

Breck slid into the booth across from Barnabas, his eyes on his friend and employer. Something was going on with him and it wasn't what had happened to Branigan.

"Breck? You tracked me down for a reason, other than to stop me from hitting the bookstore."

"You still can. I figured that was where you were heading. Amy told me you had come to town."

Barnabas grinned. Amy was his secretary and like Doc's wife and her sister, Anna, she tended to mother all fourteen of the men who resided in the Foundation building and now mothered the five ladies who had become part of the family

"She keeps track of me, I must say."

"She does, but not overboard on it. She's concerned about Branigan, she said." Breck looked up with a quick word of thanks as a plate of food slid in front of him. He was not surprised that he didn't have to order. They ate there enough the owner had memorized what they usually had.

"Me, too. It was typical of him to do what he did. All of us would have." Barnabas sipped at his coffee before continuing. "But that's not why you tracked me down."

"No, I talked to Alice and then Dallas. There was a package left on the doorstep of Brett's office building. Brett found it this morning on Guenivere's desk. I guess the responding officers placed it there. After what had happened, he didn't open it but called in Alice." He paused, his face growing stern. "It contained dead roses and a photo of Guenivere and her mom from the day before. Brett is ready to lock them away."

"A threat, but why? How does it have to do with what happened?"

"That's what Will wants to know. He's going to have Dallas or Alice talk with Guenivere. Brett said something happened years ago that affected Guenivere. She never said what and when they asked, she just shook her head and walked away."

"I got the sense from her that she is hiding something way down deep." Barnabas sighed. "All the ladies did or tried to."

"They don't want to worry us. That's a given." Breck paused, a slice of toast in his hand that he was staring at. "Why did I have toast?"

Barnabas began to laugh. "You could have said no, but you wouldn't, not wanting to offend." He sobered. "What are we to do? Did Will ask anything of us?"

"Not of us. Branigan. He's made a connection with her that her father says she has never had with any of the young men of her acquaintance. She just hadn't wanted to go out with them or be seen with them other than in a group and that not very often. He told Alice that for Branigan to be able to hold her hand and for her not to break their contact was not his daughter. But he was glad to see her reaching out. He said at times she seems to have no hope."

Barnabas nodded, a frown appearing on his face as he stared at the man sitting down the cafe from him, who seemed to be focused on him. Just why, he had no idea. He didn't recognize him. He sighed as he pulled out his phone, snapping a quick picture and sending it on to Dallas before he glanced at the text message that had arrived. He paled.

Breck looked up at the muttered exclamation from Barnabas and then stood, the bill in his hand as he walked through the cafe on Barnabas' heels

"Barnabas?"

Breck's voice stopped Barnabas who stood, his eyes back on the text message.

"It's Brett. He just received a death threat. This time aimed at Lena and himself." Barnabas looked around. "Someone is out here, Breck. They're watching us. Why?"

"It has to with Branigan?" Breck shook his head. "Listen, I'll head that way and then to find Branigan."

Barnabas nodded, his eyes searching his friend's face. "I agree. The bookstore doesn't need my money today. I'm heading back to the office. I'll see what I can find out." He was away before Breck could say anything or do anything other than to just stand and watch his friend stride rapidly away from him.

Chapter 8

Lena stood back from their front door, pointing to the living room as Breck stood outside. He had not wanted to come, had not wanted to tell them what had been found, but Brett had asked him to.

"Lena? It's been a while. How are you?"

She sighed, and he could see the fine lines of strain in her face. "I have been better. Come on into the kitchen. There's a fresh pot of coffee and it's near lunchtime. You'll stay, of course." She headed down the hallway, hesitating for a moment at the living room doorway, her eyes on her daughter.

Guenivere had brought out her laptop, plunked herself down in her favourite chair and started to answer office emails. But now she sat, her hands idle on the closed laptop, her eyes on Branigan as he slept once more. She had risen at one point and covered him with the afghan her mother kept in a chest under one window before she sat back down. Her hand had brushed his hair back into place and had lingered for a moment on his cheek, a prayer rising for healing from him.

Breck watched as well, before he shook his head. He knew Branigan, knew his heart, about as well as he had let anyone in. He had driven himself to help solve the mysteries surrounding their five friends, working long hours on it. He had worn himself out, Breck supposed, before he moved on to the kitchen, to reach for the mug of coffee he was handed and then taking a seat at the round oak table.

Rising once more, he reached for the tray Lena had in her hands, heading for Guenivere. He set the tray on the coffee table, turning to find Guenivere watching him, a puzzled look on her face.

"I'm sorry. I didn't mean to startle you." He grinned at the look she shot him.

"No, that's okay. I have it happen all the time." She sighed. "Nothing is easy anymore, and I dislike that."

"Something I can do to help?"

She shook her head. "Not unless you can trace some emails for me. They're threatening somewhat in nature. I don't want to go to Dad. He'll lock me away somewhere." Guenivere was grumbling and she knew it.

Breck perched himself on a chair near her. "I can but so can one of our friends who is an IT specialist."

"He is? Oh wonderful." She thrust the laptop at him. "Here. Take this. The password is Truck."

"Truck?" He grinned at that.

"Yes. Truck. Too obvious I know, but it is what it is."

"Breck? When did you get here?'

Neither of his companions in the room had realized that Branigan was awake and had been listening to the conversation, a frown on his face despite the headache or because of it, he couldn't decide. Good, he thought. She's reaching out. That's what I want to see.

"Branigan! How are you feeling?" Breck shifted to look around at him, finding Branigan watching Guenivere, who had suddenly discovered something interesting on her hands and was refusing to look at him. Breck bit back his grin. Here we go again, Lord. Only this time, please? We don't want to almost lose either one of them. It's been too close with all of them.

"Like I was run over by a car. How am I supposed to feel?" He shook his head slightly, finding the headache better. "What are you doing here?"

"I'm supposed to be having lunch here. Or at least, I was asked." He pointed at the tray. "Lena sent that in for you."

Branigan sat up and then stood, reaching for the tray. "We'll eat in the kitchen. We don't need to make more work for her." He walked away, not hearing the muted sound from Guenivere.

Breck spun back, his eyes narrowed as he watched her. "Go. Tell him not to make decisions for you. You can make your own."

She shook her own head. "No, he's right. Mom shouldn't have." She made to rise, stopped when Breck's hand was laid on her arm.

"No. It was your decision where you ate. If you want to eat out there, fine. If you had wanted to eat in here, that would have been okay. Find your voice. Tell him how you feel." He laughed at the look on her face, a look of shock and disbelief. "Trust me. He can take it. We've all had conversations with him at some point or other, sometimes at the top of our voices. Surprised you with that, didn't I? He cares about us and that's why he's like he is. I can see he's concerned about you. How far it will go, only God knows. Trust Him to lead you two. But don't be afraid to speak up."

Once more, Guenivere felt hope rising in her. "You're right, Breck, but I don't want to hurt his feelings or get him mad at me." She jumped as she felt an arm around her shoulders and then Branigan perched on the arm of her chair, a thank you mouthed to Breck.

"Is that what happened, love? Someone got extremely angry with you and put you down?" He waited until a hesitant nod came. "I'm not like that. Breck's right. I sometimes step in where I shouldn't and take over. Don't let me. I don't care if you yell at me. Scream at me. Shove me. Hit me. I can take it all." His arm tightened, his only thought in how to make her understand.

None of the three saw Lena hovering in the shadows of the hallway just outside the door, a hand to her mouth, blinking rapidly to clear away the tears. All this time, Lord, and we never knew. She just refused to tell us. Lord, help us to help her. Don't let her get put down again. Not like that. I sense that Your leading here, bringing Branigan and the rest of the Foundation guys as we call them into her life. I pray that she can make friends with their ladies. They can help her in ways that I or her father can't.

Chapter 9

A week later, Branigan had moved back to his apartment, albeit it very reluctantly. He knew he would be unable to have the contact with Guenivere that he had had, that he had come to enjoy. He would make a point of seeing her every day, he decided. Just how that would work out, he wasn't sure.

He turned as he heard footsteps and his friends, Baird and Blair, approached. Blair pointed towards the sitting area at one side of the lobby. The Foundation Building housed the men, Doc and Anna, and also had offices for each one, as well as a well-stocked infirmary. The lobby was larger than most buildings, and had a sitting area on each side of the door, with gas fireplaces facing one another.

Branigan sat, relieved to be off his feet. He had been on the run all day, he thought, catching up on the tasks and security plans that had sat on his desk for the last few days. He still had some to work through, but he felt better about what was there.

"Branigan? How are you feeling now you're home and back to work?" Baird watched him closely, seeing something different about his friend.

Branigan shrugged. "All right, I guess. I've made a dent into the work on my desk." He paused, not sure how to continue. "Have you heard anything from Will or Alice?"

Blair shook his head. "Not a thing. They won't unless they need to talk to us." He shared a look with Baird, the two men and their wives, Berneen and Devaney having spoken about Branigan and Guenivere. "How's Guenivere?"

Branigan shrugged. "I haven't talked to her today, so I am not sure. I plan on calling her later. Why?" He looked between the two, eyes narrowing as he tried to determine what they were up to, and they were up to something, they had that look about them.

"Berneen asked if she would be willing to come for dinner one night. She's seen her around church, is in the same evening Bible study group with her, and has wanted to get to know her better. With you involved with her, she thinks it's a perfect opportunity."

"Devaney feels the same, Branigan." Blair held up a hand as Branigan went to protest. "We're not prying or interfering in your life. It's just that Devaney has picked up on something with Guenivere. You know how her instincts are after having lived on the streets for so long. She's worried about her."

Branigan sat back, his eyes on the dark hardwood floor and then nodded. "There is something, but she hasn't shared it all with me. I'm getting bits and pieces. It's not just what happened to us. There's something else, something I don't feel right sharing until I've talked to her and had her permission to bring you in on it. And that I would like to do. We work together well as a team, all of us, ladies included, and I think that's what is going to be needed. I fear for her. For her life. For her sanity." He groaned. "Did I really say that?"

"You did. I gather she has had something happen that has affected her in ways she has hidden. We all do that." Blair stood, seeing Devaney hesitating near the doorway. "I have to run, but talk to your lady. Let her know we'd like to have her for dinner. Either just you two or some of the rest of us. Maybe ask her to our potluck on Sunday."

Branigan stared after him as he walked away, hearing Baird snickering near him. "Not funny, Baird."

"Actually, it is. Now you know how we felt."

Branigan dropped his head to hide his smile. "Yeah, I guess I do. Sort of. How did you do it, Baird. You and Berneen married under duress but you survived everything, growing to love her so deeply. How?"

"God. That's the only way, Branigan. Berneen had been beaten down just by being held captive. She has often told me she was afraid she would never be free, but when she saw me, she knew God had sent someone. When you dragged her away with me, she fought you, but down deep inside, she was glad we had."

Branigan sat back, mulling over what Baird had said, his hand absentmindedly rubbing at his cheek, touching a fading bruise. "I can see that. She had Darby to worry about as well." He paused, gathering his thoughts, knowing that what he would say would go no further. "Did you hear about the parcel that had been left that day? Dead roses and picture of Guenivere and her mom. Who does that?"

"I would suspect it's related to the man who was there. I heard from Barnabas that he's been taken to another district where he's facing murder charges. God had His hand on you two that day."

"He did." Branigan looked up as he heard the door open and then was on his feet, moving towards it. Guenivere had appeared, and he could tell she was distraught.

Guenivere paused inside the doorway, her mouth dropping open as she took in the welcoming foyer, searching for a board that would show where Branigan's apartment was. Not seeing one, she looked further, finding the security desk tucked away unobtrusively near the elevators. She had taken a couple of steps that way when arms swept around her and pulled her into a tight hug. Branigan, she thought. She turned, her own arms around him as she tried to compose herself.

"Guenivere? You're here?" Branigan turned her back towards where he had been sitting. Baird had stood, watching them closely. "Here. Sit. What's wrong?"

Guenivere sank down, grateful to be off her feet, grateful for Branigan's arm around her.

"I had to come." She thrust her phone at him. "Swipe it and then take a look at the picture." Tears welled in her eyes, tears she refused to let fall.

Branigan reached for her phone, his eyes not leaving her, hearing Baird muttering something. He heard footsteps approaching, that stopped short of where they were.

He finally looked down at her phone, staring at the picture. "It's us, from that day. Someone else was there."

"There was. I didn't see anyone but someone had to leave that parcel. It wasn't that man. I watched him walk up to the door. He didn't have anything."

"So, someone left the parcel when you weren't in the reception area?" Baird had spoken up, startling Guenivere, who shrank back against Branigan for a moment.

"They have to have. I was working in the one office for a while and was back and forth. They could have left it at any time that morning." She sighed. "We'll never know, now will we?"

Branigan looked past her to see Buckley and Benen standing there before they approached and sat as well. Guenivere stared at them, not sure if she wanted them there or not. But, after all, Buckley was their pastor or minister or whatever you wanted to call him. She guessed to herself that if she and Branigan really were dating that she would have to get to know his friends. Suddenly she felt alive, wanted, loved, and ready to face whatever it was.

"Guenivere? Can we talk with the others? Can I tell them what you have shared? If you say no, that's fine. I'll work on it, but having the others take a look at it will help."

She shrugged, her face turning to him, seeing the concern on his face as well as something just for her alone in his eyes. She nodded. "I think so, Branigan. It's time. It may all be related somehow."

"That's what I was going to suggest." Benen spoke up. "Listen, it's near supper time. I know Cadee has planned a barbecue for us. Join us, Guenivere." He laughed at the look she threw Branigan. "Yeah, he can tag along, if he really must." He laughed harder as Branigan spluttered out some unintelligible words. "Buckley, you're free, you said."

"I can't put her to all that work." Guenivere was horrified at the thought.

"Trust me. She loves doing this. In case you had forgotten, she worked on a mission field with her parents. They were used to putting on big meals. She has told me she misses that." He looked past her. "And there she is. Cadee? Have you met Guenivere?"

"I have." Cadee reached to hug Guenivere, pulling her to her feet. "You're staying for supper. I won't take no for an answer. And then we will talk. I want to know what it is that's been going on with you. I can sense you're having an adventure. All of us like to tag along on those." Her arm linked with Guenivere, she led her away, leaving the men staring after her before Buckley started to laugh.

"Well, I guess that settles it. What do we need to do to help?"

"If I know Cadee, likely not much." Benen rose, following after the two ladies, leaving Branigan lost in thought.

"Branigan?"

Buckley's quiet voice broke through to the other man and he turned, a sudden look of understanding on his face.

"I think I know where this is going. I have a feeling I know who. I've seen him watching her, not realizing what was going on."

"Do you have a name?" Buckley's eyes widened as Branigan spoke again rapidly. "We'll need to prove that. You'll need to find out from Guenivere if that is indeed who it is. I suspect you are correct in your surmising. I have seen him around town. All the girls and younger ladies avoid him."

"They do? I missed that." Branigan was quiet as they headed for Benen's apartment, Buckley tapping at the door and then opening it, hearing Cadee and Guenivere's laughter spilling out towards them.

"I haven't heard her laugh like that. Thank you, Cadee. And thank you, Lord. She needs friends like these ladies."

Cadee finally turned to Guenivere, their meal over and the remnants put away. The two ladies had taken over the couch, one on each end, their feet under them, laughing at the nonsense that Buckley was coming up with. His comments were getting more outrageous the more they laughed.

Finally, Benen bought into the conversation, watching Cadee for a moment before she nodded.

"Buckley, can we spend some time in prayer? We are going to need all the wisdom and protection that the Good Lord can provide. I just have that feeling."

Buckley nodded, seeing the consent from the others and bowing his head, led them to the throne of God, his words bringing peace and soothing to Guenivere's sore, troubled heart.

Guenivere looked around at the four gathered with her, her eyes resting on Cadee, who was nodding, a smile of encouragement on her face. She turned suddenly, looking for Branigan who rose, came towards her and shifted her over on the couch so that he could take her spot and just wrapped her in his arms. The strength and trust in her that she felt gave her courage to speak.

Chapter 10

Guenivere kept her eyes on her hands, seeing Branigan's wrapped around hers. She tried to sort through her thoughts but wasn't very successful at that. She bit at her lip, not sure where to start.

"Start at the beginning, love. Start where is all started. You told me you were young, what 12 or so?" Branigan's quiet voice in her ear had her looking up at him before she nodded.

"I was 12. There was a group of us youth from the church that hung around together. A lot of them have left town now, finding a life elsewhere. There are still three or four around, but we don't talk much now. He destroyed that."

"Who, Guenivere? Who destroyed this group?" Benen leaned forward, his forearms resting on his knees as he intently watched her.

She shook her head, paused, and then shook it again. "I need to tell you what happened. I am almost sure that you'll be able to guess. He's made it that obvious."

"Jason Lang." Cadee's quiet voice had Guenivere's head whipping around to stare at her, even as her face paled.

"You're not from here. How did you know?"

Cadee shrugged. "Sometimes God does that. He speaks a name. I know of a lady, the wife of a police chief, who God always spoke to when their friends were going through things. She was always right. She would rather He had used someone else. I guess that what He's done here. I've seen him around. Seen him watching you when you didn't know he was there. He has an evilness about him that I can sense."

"Thank you, Cadee. No one else has ever picked up on that so quickly. He hides what he does." She paused, biting at her lip, feeling Branigan's hand on hers, squeezing lightly. "I have to go back to when I was 12, almost 13. Jason used to come to the church every once in a while, but not on a regular enough basis that we wanted him in our group. He resented that. He wanted to come in and take over, and we just wouldn't let him. I know the guys chased him away many times. The girls were all afraid of him. I have no idea what he did or didn't do or say to any of them. We never talked about it and we should have. I guess we were ashamed or something like that.

"I was riding my bike home one day from my grandparents. I usually cut through the park in town, feeling it was safe enough to do so. He was waiting for me. He must have followed me. I didn't see the wire he had strung across the path until my front wheel hit is and I flew off my bike, landing in a small pond. As I tried to drag myself up, Jason was there, his hands on my shoulders. He kept shoving me down into the water. I pleaded with him to let me go. I know I was crying. He just didn't listen.

"Jason told me that I was no good, that I was ugly, that no one would ever want to marry me. He kept repeating this every time he shoved me down into the water, until finally he made me agree with him. He shoved me back down once more and then disappeared. I crawled up the embankment and just laid there until I could get my breath back. I think I was crying but I couldn't tell, my face was so wet and muddy. All I could think of was what Mom would say when she saw me. I finally got up, found my bike and wheeled it home. The front tire was bent. I knew I had to fix it before Dad saw it or he would question me on what happened. Neither of them were home. I showered, got into some clean clothes, and threw my dirty ones in the washer, hoping to have them done before Mom got home and questioned me.

"They were late getting home that night, having been delayed by some road construction on the way. I have often wondered, if they had gotten home earlier, if I would have told them. I really don't know." She turned her face to look at Branigan, seeing a shuttered look on his face before he smiled at her. "Anyway, I drove it all down inside, as deep as I could. I couldn't talk about it. He had threatened to do something to Dad's truck or car. He also threatened to burn our house down. He said he wouldn't do anything if I kept quiet."

Cadee slid over, her arms around her new friend, holding her as the healing tears began to fall, Branigan's hand resting on her back for a moment before he rose, nodding with his head towards the balcony.

"Branigan? Did you suspect this?" Buckley's voice was quiet, they were all in shock at what she had said. "She was too young."

"She was. She has let some things slip. I had a suspicion that's who it was." He sighed, running his hands through his hair, and then gripping the balcony railing tight enough they turned white. "I want him. I want him for what he did to Guenivere. Who knows what all he's done to the others."

"Makes me wonder if that's why they moved away. He hasn't." Benen looked back through the patio doors. "Cadee will talk with her, find out anything more she can, and then ask permission to share it with us. We need to get him, Branigan, for her sake and for the others."

"That man who ran you down? How is he connected to Lang?" Buckley's question had the men stopping any motion before they stared at one another.

"I wonder. I need to talk to Alice or Dallas or Will. I know we can't do anything about the past. But I want this cleared up. Guenivere deserves to live the life that she should have had and didn't." He paused, sorrow flickering across his face. "Brett and Lena will be devastated when they hear, and hear they must. Whoever it was behind that man hasn't stopped. I have seen evidence on their security system that someone matching his description has been lurking around the building."

"But I thought he had been taken to another town?" Benen was puzzled.

"He was. Will called me late this afternoon. He escaped custody somehow and they think he headed back this way. That was three days ago." Branigan turned to the doors, ready to race to Guenivere's side but knowing she needed the time with Cadee. "They think he's come back here, ready to seek revenge."

"And that puts you in danger, do you know that?" Buckley's hand on Branigan's shoulder stopped his forward motion. "We need to bathe you two in prayer. It's going to get ugly, uglier than it has already."

Chapter 11

Later that night, Branigan followed Guenivere as she drove home, not willing to let her go on her own. He parked on the street and was at her car door before she could open it, his hand reached out for hers.

"Branigan, I'm sorry. I shouldn't have talked." She was contrite, ashamed at what she had said.

His finger under her chin raising it so he could see it clearly in the street light, Branigan shook his head.

"No, the time is right for this to be settled. You have lived too much of your life in the shame and shadows of his words and actions. You did nothing to deserve that treatment. I want to see the bright, vibrant, beautiful lady that I care a lot for live her life as she should and as God would want her to."

She reached to hug him before she stepped back. "Do you think we'll catch him?"

Branigan nodded. "I can guarantee you we will. All the guys will be working on this. Ennis', Bradon's wife, cousin is a detective in the next town. He'll want to be involved. We need to talk to Will or Dallas or Alice, I think. What he has done continues to affect the town. We don't know who all he's gone after."

"That's my fear, Branigan. I had a friend commit suicide when we were 16. I know she was really afraid

———

60

of him, would go out of her way to avoid him. I don't know that we can prove he was behind that or not."

"Let me have her name, and we'll look into it." He wrapped her into a hug again. "Come on. Let's get you inside. I don't like you out here."

She nodded as they walked to the door, his arm still around her. Thank You, Lord. You heard my pleas and begging and brought someone in who is strong enough to stand up to him. Just don't let him get hurt any more than he was.

Branigan watched the house, waiting for the lights to go out, his fingers tapping at the steering wheel, his phone on the seat beside him. He had called Will, letting him know he wanted to speak with him. Would tomorrow do? Will had asked him to come over that night, even late, knowing that Branigan would not be calling him and asking for that if it wasn't serious.

Will sat across from Branigan at his kitchen table, his hand wrapped around a mug, waiting for Branigan to speak. When he had, Will sat back, nodding.

"That explains a lot we could never understand. Why did so many of that group leave town. I know who she means about the friend committing suicide. She's not the only one, unfortunately. There have been at least three others that we know of, but we were never satisfied they killed themselves."

"You think he did it and made it look like they did." Branigan sat back, his thoughts muddled for a moment. "That makes me worry even more for Guenivere."

"Let me ask you a question, Branigan. You don't have to answer if you don't want to. I know it would have been a question your father would be asking."

Branigan nodded once more, his thoughts drifting to his father. His mother had died in childbirth, his baby sister not living past a few days. His father had been the one to raise him on his own, before kidney disease had struck and taken him too soon and too young. Branigan had just finished high school in his home town in PEI. He had been at loose ends for a few months, finally enrolling in college. When he had been approached by Barnabas and offered employed with the Foundation, he had jumped at the chance, eager to get away from the memories that haunted him.

"Go ahead."

"I have seen you two together. You make each other whole. She is your heart, Branigan, whether you realize it yet or not. I have seen her watch you, seeing the hope in her eyes. She trusts you in a way I have never seen her trust anyone before. Watch her heart. That's all I ask."

Branigan nodded. "You're right, Will. She is all that. We've talked. She's been reluctant to go forward with our friendship, I think because of Lang. She has more she hasn't said about what happened and what he told her. You'll likely find he has threatened her family, her friends and any boyfriend she might have." He paused, groaning as his phone chimed, excusing himself to pull it out. It was late, after ten o'clock, and he didn't know of anyone who would be calling him.

Guenivere's voice flooded over his phone, her words mingling together in a manner that he couldn't understand. He was on his feet, heading for the door, Will at his heels.

"It's Guenivere. I can't make out what's wrong."

Will pointed to his car. "I'll drive. We'll get your car later." His phone was out and he was calling for backup at the Danby's, not sure what they would find.

Guenivere stood, her arms wrapped around herself, giving her statement, when she saw Branigan standing, waiting for her. She flew across the yard into his arms, as fast as her feet would take her, sobs shaking her body.

Will stood for a moment before he turned to the responding officer, trying to determine what had transpired. He frowned when he heard, his eyes finding Branigan and nodding.

Branigan's arms tightened on Guenivere before he led her to Will's car, lifting her up to sit on the trunk, leaning against it himself, his back to the house.

"Guenivere? What happened? I couldn't make out what you were saying."

She was still shaking. "He was in the house. I don't know how, but I heard him moving around downstairs. I called you instead of the police. I'm sorry. I shouldn't have done that."

"No, you did right. I was with Will, discussing something, when you called. He called it in on our way here. Did Lang find you?"

Guenivere shook her head. "No, he didn't make it up the stairs. I heard the sirens and then heard the front door slam." She looked back at the house. "Mom and Dad are away for the next few days. I don't want to stay here. Not on my own. That's something else he's taken from me." She could feel the anger growing within her.

"I'll take you out to the Foundation building. There are suites there you can use for now. We have security on site, so he won't get to you in the building."

Will stood listening, nodding as he heard Branigan's words. "That's a good idea, Guenivere. Your father would agree."

She sighed. "I know he would." She glanced past him at the house. "I have to get some things. Can I go in?"

"Give us about twenty minutes. I want you to walk through with me. And yes, Branigan can go with you." He grinned at the look she threw him.

Branigan laughed at her muttered comment that everyone seemed to be making them a couple, did he know that?

"I would like that, Guenivere. I would like that a lot. But we have time. We'll talk." He reached to brush the hair back from her cheek, her eyes on his, hope in them, he thought. "We'll talk and figure it out. Right now, we need to get you safe. I came with Will.

He'll take us back to his place and I'll grab my car. He'll have someone follow us, that I know without him saying a word.

Chapter 12

Two weeks later, Guenivere rose from her desk in the office building, heading for the work building as it was called, intent on finding Douglas. She had an invoice for work on a vehicle that she didn't recognize

"Douglas?"

"Right here, Guenivere. What's up? You look like you're on a mission." Douglas grinned at her, wiping his hands on a rag he stuffed into his back pocket. "What do you have there?"

"This. An invoice for work. I don't recognize the vehicle. It's not one of ours, but it says you worked on it."

"Let's see." Douglas frowned. "No, that's not one of ours. And I didn't work on it. I would have signed off on it, and it isn't signed. Now, who?"

"Lang. It has to be him."

"Jason Lang?" When Guenivere nodded, Douglas sighed. "I've seen him hanging around here at times. Whenever I approached, he ran. Your Dad knows he's been here. I talked to Alice and she was going to talk to Will, to see what they could do."

"There's not much we can do. I just don't understand how the invoice ended up on my desk. It wasn't there yesterday and I pulled these first thing this morning. It was there then."

Douglas shook his head. "We need to talk to that boyfriend of yours and see if he can find out if the security system has been tampered with. I suspect it was."

"My boyfriend?" She turned to face him. "Just who do you mean?"

"Branigan. Isn't he your beau?"

She groaned. "You, too? What is it with everybody?"

Douglas stopped her before hugging her. "I've seen the two of you together. You make a couple, cute couple at that. We're glad for you, Guenivere. That's all."

"Thank you, Douglas. Now to track him down and talk to him."

Branigan stood later that day, his eyes on the security feed from overnight. Then he saw the man approaching the building, a key in his hand, reaching to turn off the security system before he was back resetting everything and then locking the door behind him. Brett stood beside him, shock on his face.

"How did he get a key and the security code?"

Branigan strode over to the panel, a grim look on his face, before he pried off the cover.

"Here. This is not part of the control panel." He pointed towards what seemed to be a small camera. "He's placed this sometime the office was empty. It wouldn't have taken long. I can almost guarantee you it leads to a computer somewhere."

"I'm sure it does." Brett turned. "Guenivere, call it in, please. Branigan, it's not your fault. We'll need to replace that, I gather, and also the locks."

"You do. I'll have to slip away and grab another control panel. Stay safe."

Two hours later, Branigan stood, watching as both Brett and Guenivere changed their passcodes. He had talked to Will, who had sent out a crime scene tech. Together they had searched the office and warehouse, finding a number of cameras hidden away. They had also found some hidden outside. That worried Branigan. He didn't think it was Lang that had done that, but who? He had put in a call to Baird, asking if he would set up a meeting for the men at the building that night. He needed their help.

Guenivere stepped away from the control panel, fear running through her. She jumped as she felt arms coming around her and then leaned back against Branigan. He made her feel safe, she decided, and that was what she needed at that very moment.

Brett watched the two closely, a frown on his face as he looked past them. Douglas stood at the door, beckoning him. He walked towards him, the office door closing quietly behind him. Brett took a look at the new lock and smiled to himself. Branigan had been adamant that they get a high quality lock with a keypad.

"Douglas?" Brett walked towards the picnic table under the nearby trees. "Something's wrong?"

Douglas sat, rubbing at the back of his head. "There is, and I don't know what. Did Guenivere tell you about the invoice? Of course, she did. That's why the activity." He drifted off in deep thought for a moment. "Do you remember that company that tried to become partners with you?"

"The Grayson Trucks. I do. They seemed to disappear from the area." Brett paused. "You're telling me that they're back?"

"I found out from a cousin that they never left the area. They went underground. He said the rumour at the time was they wanted to come in with you and use your company as a cover for their activities. For some reason, he has connected Jason Lang to them."

"It all comes back to him, doesn't it?" Brett sighed, his hands rubbing together. "Guenivere has finally told us what happened all those years ago. I wish she had told us then, but as a young teenager, she was scared. He played on that. She said he had threatened everyone she knew."

"He did, Dad." The men looked up to see the young couple standing near them. "I found dead animals on my way to school or the library or to a friend's. He made sure I knew it was from him."

"Guenivere, I wish you had told us, but I can understand why you didn't." Brett watched Branigan closely. "Branigan, this is out of our league, Douglas and I. We can watch to a certain extent when Guenivere's here on site, but we can't be with her all the time."

"I know. I have a meeting set up with my friends for tonight. We'll do some brainstorming and see what we can come up with." He looked down at Guenivere.

"Barnabas called me when I was out getting the new control panel. He has offered Guenivere an apartment in the building until this is over."

Guenivere twisted to look up at him. "He did?" She looked over at her father, seeing the relief on his face. "Dad? Do you think I should?"

"Perhaps. I would like to see you stay safe and at home but if going there means you do stay safe, then your mother and I would agree with Barnabas."

Douglas had been listening intently. "It would help, Guenivere, but it may also make it worse. If he can't get to you, then he may go after your parents."

"Barnabas thought of that. He'll be talking to you, Brett, but he has offered some of the security men and ladies that we have on site. One to be with you. One of the ladies to be with Lena."

Brett breathed a sigh of relief. "That would work. I know Lena would be agreeable." He looked down, his heart sorrowing for his daughter, but also praying through what they needed to do.

Guenivere slipped to the seat beside her father, her arm wrapping around his, her head leaning against it.

"I don't know what to do, Dad. I want you and Mom to stay safe. Does that mean I don't work for now?"

Douglas again spoke up. "It may be what it takes, Guenivere. We have you set up to work remotely. We can do that. If your Dad's not in the office, we just leave a sign on the door to look for me.

I can handle it. I'm sure we can set up a fax machine to forward what you need."

Guenivere looked relieved, feeling Branigan's hands resting on her shoulders. She felt the first ray of hope once again, that she hadn't felt in a long time."=

"Okay. Let's do this. I heard what you said about that company, Dad. Didn't you know they were still around?"

Brett looked surprised at her question. "No, I didn't. Did you?"

"I did. I've seen their vehicles. They're only around late at night or early in the morning, before there's much traffic." She paused, her face paling. "I just remember. Jason is related to one of them, I just can't remember how."

Chapter 13

Late that same afternoon, Guenivere walked the apartment that Branigan had led her to, her bare feet whispering against the oak hardwood floor, her eyes taking in the comfortable, inviting furnishings. She studied the walls, liking the butter cream colour of them and then looking upwards to study the lighter cream crown molding and ceilings. She turned, a smile on her face, to find Branigan watching her, leaning against the doorframe of the living room, arms folded cross his chest, one leg tucked over the other, the toes of that foot resting on the floor. His smile drew her to him and as he opened his arms, she walked in and hugged him.

"Thank you."

"Thank me? For what?"

"For this. For caring. For watching out for me." She leaned back to look up at him, seeing once more that look in his eyes that said she was special to him.

Branigan's smile widened. "It's what I do, my love. You deserve this and so much more." He dropped a kiss on her forehead. "Now, about supper. Are you hungry?"

"I didn't think I was, but I am. But I don't know that I have food here."

Branigan's hand on her arm stopped her. "You do. Cadee and Ennis took care of that for you. But

Doc and Anna have asked if we would join them. Anna says she knows you well from the toddlers' class at church."

Guenivere began to laugh, her eyes lighting up with amusement. "Oh, we do. We have such fun with them. Have you ever tried to carry on a conversation with a two year old?"

Branigan laughed as well, as taking her hand, he led her from her apartment, locking the door and handing her the key. "I can't say that I have. It will have to go on my bucket list."

"You would be good in that age group." She laughed even harder. "Although, with you being so tall, I don't know that you would fit into one of their chairs."

He grinned at her lightheartedness. "I can always sit on the floor. What do I need to become part of your team?"

She stopped short in Doc and Anna's hallway to stare up at him. "You're serious, aren't you? Talk to Buckley. He'll walk you through what you need to do." She looked around to find Anna standing near her. "I just found a new recruit for our class, Anna."

"You have? Wonderful. Now, come. The roast and the fixings are all ready to eat."

The next morning, Guenivere looked around the office she had set up, a mug of tea in her hand as she studied the office in the apartment. Whoever designed these had put a lot of thought into them, she thought, raising the mug to her mouth to sip from it. She grinned suddenly, thinking of what had happened earlier.

Barnabas had dropped in, just to welcome her to the building he said, and to make sure she felt safe and secure, and had everything that she needed. He had dropped a set of keys on the desk, telling her that they were for the gym, if she wanted that. She had nodded eagerly. She was a runner and cyclist, and knew that going outdoors to do that would be a foolish risk. He had stayed for a few minutes, finally walking away, calling back that he welcomed her to the family. He had just laughed at her cry of disbelief and closed the door behind him.

Guenivere shook her head. Just maybe she would be part of the family one day. She felt that was where it was heading with Branigan, but she wasn't sure. She had been beaten down for so long, she didn't really trust her instincts where men were concerned. Although Branigan was certainly changing that for her, she thought, Branigan and his friends.

She reached for her phone as it chimed, answering her mother's call. Lena had hidden her real feelings when Guenivere had told her the plans, but she was glad that her daughter was safe, at least for now. She had parted the sheer curtains on their front window that morning to see the same vehicle parked across the street, the man obviously watching their house. Alice had been by and taken down the information, promising to deal with it.

Late that afternoon, Guenivere opened up the last work email she had planned to deal with, her hand freezing as she read it, her face growing white. She shoved violently backwards from her desk, her chair clattering to the floor as she fell with it. She lay still for a moment, horror growing within her. The knock at the door had her spinning and then on her feet, racing for it, throwing it open and then throwing herself into Branigan's arms.

Branigan's arms closed around his lady as he stared down at her head before he looked sideways at Benen and Cadee. Something had happened and he wanted to find out, but first he had to calm his sweetheart down, and that was exactly what she had become. His sweetheart.

"Guenivere? What happened?" He moved her gently into the apartment, the door closing behind Benen and Cadee.

Benen strode through, looking for something, anything that would explain her reaction. He paused in the office as he saw the overturned chair. He reached to right it, his eyes stopping at the computer monitor. Not wanting to intrude or read something that was business related, he hesitated.

Guenivere stood in the doorway. "Read it. I can't."

Benen glanced over at her, seeing her nod and then turned back to read the email. His face grew grim as he read it, nodding to Branigan who had walked over.

"This is brutal, Branigan. Who is this guy?" Benen had heard some of the story but not what had happened the previous day.

"He's stalking her for some reason. I had to swap out the security system control panel yesterday. He had managed to get into the office. Will sent out a tech and during the sweep we found cameras in both buildings and outside as well. He had even managed to get a key cut."

"He did what?" Benen's voice exploded in anger, although he kept it low. He shot a glance back towards the doorway. "Cadee's has her in another room. What do we do?"

"We find him. But Guenivere remembered that he was cousins or something like that to a trucking company that tried to become partners when she was young." He paused. "I wonder if it was around the same time that she was attacked." His phone out, he was quickly dialling through to Brett.

"The timing for that company?" Brett had difficulty following Branigan's words. "Slow down, Branigan. I'm having trouble following you."

"I wondered how old Guenivere was when they tried to buy into yours."

"Guenivere? About 11 or so. That's right, it was about four months before she turned 12." Brett's voice died away. "That's why."

"To get you to come to terms? Possibly. Listen. Guenivere pulled up an email just before I got here. It's brutal, to say the least. It threatens your buildings, your trucks, you and Lena. Doesn't say anything about threatening Guenivere." Branigan listened for a moment before he nodded. "That's my plan. I'll send it on to Dallas and Will. Let them look at it. They'll be around more than likely to talk with you." He pocketed his phone, his face thoughtful.

"We didn't get to meet last night, Branigan. The guys are assembling after supper in the conference room. You know the one. Where we always meet to figure out the adventures."

"Right, we didn't." He reached to print the email, before sending it on as he had promised Brett. "I want to show them this. I don't know how much information we have, but we'll work through it and see where we go."

"Cadee offered to stay with Guenivere if she likes. The other ladies are around as well."

"That's good." Branigan turned for the doorway. "She needs that. She needs to hear their stories and know that she's not on her own." He paused, his phone out. "There is one person I think may be more than able to help us."

"Emma?" At Branigan's nod, Benen agreed. "Send on what you can. I know she'll help. She told me that when Brady and Fynn were going through what they were."

Chapter 14

Her eyes huge, Guenivere stared around at the five ladies seated in her living room, not really believing what they had said.

"There is no way on earth you have gone through this. You couldn't have."

The ladies laughed before Berneen spoke up.

"We did. God got us through that. We have had to learn to trust Him in ways we never would have. I think that's what you are learning."

Guenivere nodded. "I am. Having heard what happened to you five, it gives me confidence that God really does listen."

"He does." This from Ennis. "I know He does." She looked around at the other ladies. "We need to meet on a weekly basis, I think, for prayer, if only for prayer. I would like to start a Bible study, but for now, we need to support one another and really support Guenivere and Branigan. They are a cute couple, you know."

The ladies laughed even as Guenivere blushed. That was what she was thinking of them as, but with Lang hanging over her, she just didn't see how it would work out, not without Branigan getting hurt again.

A hand gripped hers and a soft voice spoke. "Leave it with God, Guenivere. I know it's hard, but trust Him."

Guenivere looked up at Fynn. "It is hard. It's hard to trust in someone you can't see, isn't it?"

They all agreed before six heads bowed and they raised up each other to God's throne. They left shortly after they had finished, Guenivere wandering through her apartment, to pull open the French door to the balcony and finding a chair to sit in, to watch the setting of the sun over the lake. She felt at peace, the first time in weeks, no years, she thought. No matter what happened, she would trust and leave her hand in God's.

She rose when she heard the doorbell, opening it find Branigan standing there, arms open to enfold her. Breck stood beside him as did Burnie, another friend of Branigan's.

"Can we come in, my love? We need to talk to you." Branigan's voice was sober as he asked, eyes searching her face.

"Sure. Can I get you anything?"

"No, we're fine, Guenivere. We just need to go over something with you. I'm not sure if you have met Burnie yet."

"I have. His books ship through Dad's company."

"Nice to see you out here, Guenivere. I wish the circumstances were different." Burnie's voice was soft as he spoke, finding a seat in a chair in the living room.

"They aren't, are they? But I know God has allowed this. We just have to wait on Him, I guess."

She turned to Breck. "You said you needed to talk to me?

"We do. We have had a long discussion on what it going on. We know it's only going to get worse, as I am sure you have surmised. We're pulling names and dates and addresses and whatever we can find on that company and on Lang. He is a cousin to one of the owners. Branigan talked to your Dad earlier, asking when the trucking company tried to buy into his. It was about four months before you turned 12."

They watched as her face paled and understanding dawned on her. "It was because of them? All along? That's why he did it? To get Dad to come to terms. Only I never said anything, and they had to wait." She stared past Breck for a moment before her eyes turned back to him, determination beginning to colour her face. "Of course. That would be why. But now? Why come back? Why break in and set up what they did? And the man who showed up that day? How is he involved?"

"That's what we working on." Branigan's hand tightened on the one of hers he was holding. "Fynn has a friend who is really good at finding things. I took the liberty of contacting her and asking her to research it."

Guenivere stared at him for a moment before her brow cleared. "Emma?"

"Yes, Emma. You know her?"

She nodded. "I have met her. It's Leah that I know better. Our fathers connected through the Christian trucking company organization. In fact, Branigan, her husband, Joseph, was the one who came in and set up the security system." She frowned. "He is as good as you are. How did it get hacked?"

"That's what we want to know. I'm not sure we have that information yet." Breck spoke up. "I called him in. I'll talk to him tomorrow." He stood as did Burnie. "Let us know if you get anything more, not matter how minor. Sometimes that is all it takes."

"That's what Will said. He had a detective, Dallas, come out and talk to me. Right now, there's not a lot they can do."

"No, there isn't. We have to connect the dots for them. Trust me, we will." Burnie said good night at that point, walking away with Breck, leaving Branigan to wrap Guenivere in his arms.

"Are you okay?"

She shrugged. "I'm not sure how to feel, to tell you the truth."

"Sounds about normal to me."

Branigan stood inside his doorway a short time later. He hadn't stayed as long as he would have liked to, seeing the fatigue on his lady's face. His head went back against the door as he first prayed, and then thought through what had happened. A grim determination filled him. He would track down Lang and bring him in, on his own if he had to. This needed to be over for Guenivere, he thought. It's gone on too long.

Chapter 15

Two days later, Branigan stood in the shadows of a building, watching intently as the man he had been following stopped in front of a business before he entered. His phone out, Branigan took a quick picture of the place and sent it on to Brennen and Brandon, knowing they were home and could work on discovering more about it.

He watched as the man left and walked past him before he stepped out and followed, his eyes searching for anyone following him. He could see the arrogance of the man in front of him just by how he was walking. He heard the sound of a motor and stepped back into a doorway, noting the unmarked cruiser pull up in front of the man and halt his footsteps. Alice stepped out from the passenger's side as the officer stepped out from the other, hands on their police issue weapons. Alice spoke with the man, and Branigan could see the anger flying at them from him.   A sudden move towards his pocket had the male officer shoving him against the cruiser as a knife clattered to the grounds. Handcuffs snapped around his wrists and he was shoved into the back seat through the door Alice had opened.   Branigan continued to watch from the shadows, seeing Alice looking around, almost as if she knew he was there.

Branigan waited until they left before he headed back towards his truck, his phone out to call Brennen.

"Brennen? How is it going? You have. Wonderful! What's that?" He scanned the street both ways before he ran across it, his key fob in his hand to unlock the door. He slid onto the seat, the door closing behind him, and he reached to lock it. "Who contacted you? Oh, Jace from Emma's. That's good. They have? Okay, I have a couple of stops to make. I should be there by about four." He laughed as Brennen commented that Guenivere had shown up that morning, determined to help them as best she could. "She will do that. She wants this over, and frankly, so do I. We need to find something to give her hope, and I might just have that. See you in a while."

He drove away, scanning the area around him, not seeing the delivery vehicle that had pulled out behind him and was following him. The men argued with one another as they followed Branigan through his day. They needed to find somewhere to ambush him, but they never found that opportunity. They lost sight of him mid-afternoon as the traffic picked up in town, not knowing that Branigan had finally spied them and had headed for the police department, watching for them, and then finally heading his truck for home. He was anxious to find out what his friends had discovered, but he was more anxious to find his lady and see how her day had been.

Guenivere felt an arm come around her and leaned into Branigan as he pulled a chair over with his foot and sat beside her, his eyes assessing her. She was more relaxed, feeling better about herself and where she was heading after having spent time that day with Cadee and Fynn and then spending time searching through stacks of papers she had been handed. She had stared at them and then up at Brennen, who grinned at her.

"How are you, my love?" Branigan's voice was low enough so only she could hear him.

"Okay. I think." She sat back in her chair, before she leaned against him. "Your friends are helping. They have kept me busy today." She looked around him to see Brandon watching, a grin on his face. "And Cadee and Fynn rescued me for a while. They are such fun people."

"They are. They have been through a lot on their own and then with each other. I'm happy to hear they're tracking you down. You need them. And they need you."

"And how is that?" She was puzzled at his words.

Branigan paused, realizing she didn't understand. "They need to be valued for themselves. They want to help others, to be the encouragement that person needs. Right at this moment, that person is you. Because your Dad's on the board, you know that the basis for the Foundation is to be encouragement to others. They can do that for you, and you can do that for them."

She frowned as she thought through his words before her face cleared and she nodded. "That's a wonderful thought, Branigan. The Foundation has done that for so many. Like with you all. I know you are all orphans and come from all over Canada, that Barnabas sought you out and offered you work. He didn't do that without a lot of prayer and I would gather seeking counsel. Just because all his friends had to have the same initials." She smirked as he broke out into a laugh, causing the others to raise their heads and then smile at them.

"So, my love, where do we stand?"

"I have no idea. I thought we were still sitting."

Branigan stared at her again, seeing the straight face she wore but the mischief in her eyes. He grinned. "Got me on that one. Where is the investigation at this point?"

She pointed to Brendon. "Talk to him. He and Brady and Bradon are working on something, and they won't share what they've found." Her voice was pitched at a level that the men heard and began laughing. They had been the victims of her sense of humour all day, appreciating how she could see the sunny side of life even with what she had been through.

"Okay, so, we'll talk to them." Branigan raised his voice slightly. "Guys, just an update. Alice picked up Jason Lang around noon. She doesn't know that I saw it."

"Following him, were you?" Benen grinned at him. "Let's pray he stays there or is transferred elsewhere. I found out just about ten minutes ago that he's wanted for murder in Ottawa, and they are sending a team to take him back there."

"That's good news. It will remove at least one of the players." Baird stood, stretching, before he headed for the door. He was back in short order, followed by the ladies who carried trays of food.

"Supper's here. Let's take a break and then go back at it for a while. Buckley?"

Buckley rose from where he had been sitting, a prayer for their meal rising, and then a prayer for each one in the room, specific to what they needed. Each had asked Buckley over time how he knew what to pray for them. He just shrugged and said God told him.

Finally, Barnabas rose. He had walked in just as they had started eating. He looked around at the men, thankful for each one, thankful for the ladies who were one by one joining the family, and making the men's hearts complete. His gaze rested on Branigan and Guenivere, knowing it was far from over for them, but not knowing how bad or dangerous it would get. He prayed for their safety, not knowing his prayers would be needed just a few days later.

Chapter 16

Waiting for Branigan to run back towards her after parking his truck, Guenivere shuddered, looking around, feeling something evil near her. Who or what is it, she wondered, her hand going out to grip the one Branigan extended to her. She caught his glimpse at her before he held the restaurant door open for her. It was Saturday afternoon, and he had begged her to come out for a meal with him. He promised to behave himself, a grin in place as she snorted at that idea, telling him he had no idea how to.

Finishing their meal, they lingered at the table, quiet conversation between them before Branigan rose and took her hand, tucking her tight to him as they walked back towards the truck. He settled her on the front seat and closed the door, his hand lingering for a moment on it as he watched her before he turned to walk around to his side.

The sound of running feet behind him had him turning, but not soon enough to prevent himself from slamming into the side of the truck. The breath driven from him, he stayed there as a hand shoved against his back. He couldn't see Guenivere but he had heard a sound from her.

Pulled back abruptly and then shoved into his back seat, a heavyset man following him, his assailant grabbed up the keys that had fallen and ran for the driver's side, pulling away almost before he had seated himself. Guenivere stared at him in horror, afraid to look back at Branigan. From where Branigan had been shoved, he could see her face and saw just when she determined she would not become a victim again. Just be careful, Guenivere, was his thought. They mean business. Don't do anything that would cause harm to come to you.

Branigan was with growing horror as the truck pulled to a stop in front of a locked gate. The man beside him slid out, unlocking the gate and shoving it open, shoving it closed again and setting the lock after the truck drove through, sliding back in beside him.

Branigan and Guenivere were forced from the truck this time, pushed forward towards the old mill and then up to the second floor. Branigan sought for a way out as they plodded up the steep stone steps and didn't see an opportunity to escape. He was shoved down on the floor, back to the wall and his hands bound behind him. He heard the whimper of fear from Guenivere as the same was done to her, prevented from rising by the man's hand on his head. He watched as she bent her knees and buried her head against them. Lord, we need Your help. No one will know where we are.

Guenivere felt the time passing in the coolness of the twilight that seeped into the building, causing her to shiver slightly, and by the lowering rays of the sun that she could glimpse through the broken and dirty windows, the overgrown trees helping to block the light. She heard the men arguing and knew they had stepped outside of the room, hearing the crunch of their feet on the debris and garbage that littered the stair landing and had tripped her as she stepped up. Branigan, she knew was near her. She could hear his breathing and his struggles, however quiet, to free his hands.

Branigan's hands twisted in their bonds, desperation in his movements to escape. He had to get Guenivere free, that was a given, he thought. But how? He had watched the men pace outside the room before one had thundered down the stairs. He heard the sound of his truck starting up and moving away. He knew the mill, knew how close to home he was, and knew the path back there better than most. Branigan had walked it many times, sometimes in anger, sometimes just in solitude, sometimes when he had heavy thinking to do, and other times just to find the peace from God that he only found in nature. He felt something touch his arm and jumped, looking down, finding that Guenivere had moved closer to him and rested her head against his arm.

"Are you okay?" He kept his voice as low as he could.

She nodded, her hair brushing against his chin. "I am. I know this place. It belongs to the Langs."

"It does? I've walked this way many times. I never knew."

"You wouldn't. They likely have it buried into a numbered company by now." She frowned, her eyes on the doorway. "There's only one out there now. We should be able to get away."

"We're tied up, remember?" Branigan jumped as he felt her hands on his wrists, working to release the rope. He rubbed at them when the rope dropped away before he rose and crept towards the door, eying it and the debris around it. The second kidnappers had disappeared down the stairs.

"I think if we shut the door, we can block it." Guenivere had followed him, her hand on his back. "There's another way down that not many people know about. We used to explore here when teens, partly to irritate Jason, partly because it was always good for ghost stories."

Branigan stared at her in disbelief. "Ghost stories?"

She nodded, a quick grin on her face. "Did you not do that?"

"No. I had a paper route after school and spent other time mowing grass or shovelling snow. Dad didn't want me sitting idle. He wanted me to learn to help others."

"He did right. Now, find something we can block the door with." She reached past him to grab at the door, working it inch by inch to close it. She stood against it when she was finished, watching as Branigan approached with a large branch.

"This should do, but we can move some other debris close to it. There are some larger rocks I'll grab. You go find the other entrance and make sure we can get down it." He paused, his eyes on her face, before he reached to give her a quick kiss, then moving away from her, leaving Guenivere standing, staring after him, her hand on her mouth.

Waiting across the room for Branigan, Guenivere searched for anything they could use to defend themselves, finding an iron pipe about three feet long. Her hand reached for it, and then paused, her face growing white as she backed away, right into Branigan, whose hands came up to balance her. She spun, her hand grabbing for his as she pulled him away from the area and then to the secret door. She shoved him through, pulled the door closed behind her, even as she heard pounding at the room door. Her hand pushed him down the broken stone steps and then out into the open where they were hidden by the overgrown shrubs and grass. She pointed towards the Foundation building.

"That way. We need to leave."

Branigan grabbed for her hand once more and pulled her with him, moving as silently and as rapidly as was possible until he reached the well-worn path he liked to walk. He slowed his steps, looking back over his shoulder before he looked down at her

"What was that all about? I saw you reach for the pipe and back away."

Guenivere nodded, her throat moving as she swallowed hard. "I had to. There were bones there, Branigan. And they were human."

He stopped suddenly, looking back once more before he wrapped her into a hug. "Bones? Come on. Let's run, if you can. I'm glad you're wear flat-soled shoes."

"I hadn't planned on running for our lives when I got dressed this morning. I thought a nice quiet lunch, a walk along the river or lakeshore. Not getting dumped in an old haunted mill and then finding a dead body and then running for our lives. Not once did I expect this." She was grumbling, she knew, seeing Branigan trying to hide his smile, and felt entitled to do just that.

"It's okay, my love. We're almost at the building now. About ten minutes or so." He stopped as she pulled at his hand, a question on her face.

"Branigan? What you did?" She looked up at him, her heart in her eyes for him to see.

He sighed, looking past her, biting at his lip, before he nodded. "I know. I shouldn't have kissed you. I couldn't resist."

Her hand on his cheek turned her to him. "It's okay. I just never expected it. Is that what I'm in for with you? The unexpected?"

He grinned, satisfied that she held no grudges against him doing that. "Yeah. Probably. More than likely."

"Real definite there, buster. Make up your mind." She spun and walked forward, leaving him staring after her, his mouth open before he grinned and ran to catch up with her, his hand reaching for hers, finding hers nestling into his.

I could get used to this, Lord, he thought. Is she the one? Is she the one Dad prayed for all those years? The one he wove into stories for me at bedtime as a young boy? The one he said would be my Proverbs 31 lady, my helpmeet?

Chapter 17

Breck stared at Branigan's truck and then back towards where he saw Branigan and Guenivere emerging from the woods and shook his head. Now why, he thought, are they walking and from there? He walked rapidly towards them, as Branigan looked up and waved.

"Branigan? What on earth? You two are filthy!" Breck's voice held concern and a touch of amusement for a moment until he had a closer look at their faces and sobered. "What happened?"

"We were kidnapped, dumped in the old Lang mill, found skeletal remains, and then walked back here. Isn't that enough adventure for the day?" Guenivere was frustrated and scared at the same time. She brushed past Breck and headed for the back door of the building, intent on getting cleaned up. Branigan's hand stopped her.

"Just a sec, my love. I'll walk you in." His head turned as he eyed Breck. "She's right in what she said. We need to meet, all of us. And I would like to have Will or Dallas here, if Will lets him." He pointed to his truck. "He'll need a crime scene team to go over that. Did anyone see it drive in?"

"I have no idea. I just saw it as I saw you two walking back here." Breck shook his head, his phone out as he held up a hand for them to wait. A few minutes' conversation with Will and he approached them. "Will wants you to change but put your clothes into a clean garbage bag. Your shoes as well. He'll be out here in twenty."

"Twenty? As in twenty minutes? That doesn't leave a girl much time to get cleaned up, now does it?" Guenivere broke free from Branigan and ran for the building, leaving him staring after her in frustration.

"She's terrified, Branigan, frustrated, hurt." Breck's voice caught his ear as he walked away.

Branigan spun, his hand up. "I know. I know. I just wish it was different. Sometimes I really don't know how to help her, to give her the hope she needs."

"Only God can. Pray for her. Be there for her. I sense both of you have feelings for each other, and no, I'm not prying into that. You are prayed for, you and your lady, my friend. Go. Get cleaned up. We'll meet in the conference room. I think some of the guys are already in there." Breck watched as Branigan nodded before he too headed for the building and to clean up.

Watching Will later from where he stood leaning against the wall in the conference room, Branigan kept his arm tight around Guenivere. She had sought him out, tears in her eyes as she clutched the garbage bag holding her clothes. He had taken it from her, handed it to Alice who had approached and shaking his head at her, swept Guenivere into his arms and away to a corner of the room where it was quieter.

Guenivere finally turned, her eyes on Will as he approached, sighing to herself. Now, comes the fun.

"Guenivere?   I know you've given your statement as has Branigan. Tell me."

She shook hard enough that her hair trembled before she gained control of herself. "I was looking for something to defend us. I had found that pipe. My hand was on it when I saw the bones." She stared in horror at her hand, Will watching her closely, before he looked around and beckoned Brady over.

Brady studied her and then Branigan, whose eyes were on his lady.

"Guenivere?" When she looked up at Brady, he gave her a grin. "Will's worried about you. He thinks you're shaking because you're afraid of him." As a paramedic, Brady had found that humour sometimes helped.

She glared at him for a moment before looking at Will. "No, it's that's place and that body. We used to go there as teens. It was our haunted house where we told ghost stories. I guess we shouldn't have but you know teenagers."

"I do, Guenivere. I do. Been out there a time or two myself in the last few years and felt the evil there. And that's what is there, evil. I just wanted to make sure you hadn't remembered anything else."

Guenivere's head shook as she frowned in concentration. "I don't think so. Branigan was piling stuff against the door to keep it closed and I had headed for the secret staircase. We had found it as kids and couldn't figure out why it was there."

"The mill's been there for years. Rumour had it that it was part of the Canadian route of the Underground Railway from the States."

Branigan nodded. "That would make sense. Bring them in after dark and then take them out again before it became light." He paused, a thought turning in his mind. "But who is that we found?

"Alice and Dallas are looking through missing persons' reports from here. If there is nothing there, they'll expand out to the other forces nearby. It will take a while, likely, to identify who it is. And the coroner thinks it's a male."

Guenivere paled even more. "Lang's father. He just disappeared a few years ago. No one could find him." She raised startled eyes. "Is that him?"

"That's a possibility we'll be looking at. We have a lot of footwork and investigations to do. Now, you two? Can you please stay out of trouble?" A grin covered his face for a moment before he walked away.

Chapter 18

A week later, Guenivere walked into her father's office, a sheaf of papers in her hand. She had started working out of the office again, shrugging when the protest went up. She simply stated that she was done running, that they could find her anywhere they wanted to, and had. So, why should she hide? Her mother had protested but she saw the glint of admiration in her father's eye. She knew she was scared of what could happen, but she refused to live her life in fear any more. Buckley had spent time with her over the past week, bringing up verses for her to study about trust, protection and hope. He said he had to add hope. That God had told him he had to.

Guenivere had smiled at Buckley, taken the list of verses, and had been drawn deep into a study of them. Branigan had joined her as he could, but he was run off his feet, working long hours on security systems. He had laughed but also grumbled that the jobs were cutting into their time together.

Branigan had stood silent when she told him that her decision was not to hide but to be out in the open, working back in the office. He had simply hugged her without a word, but his attitude had told her he trusted her instincts and that he would back her all the way.

Brett looked up as his daughter entered, momentarily frowning, before he reached for the papers.

"What do we have here?"

"Someone wants to set up a new contract. I'm not comfortable for some reason with them."

"Sit. Let's have a look." Brett read through the paperwork before he dropped it to his desk and sat back, studying his daughter. When did she grow up, Lord? It happened far too quickly, I think. "We'll have Branigan look into this. I agree. There is something off about it."

Guenivere nodded, before she groaned. "I know why it's so familiar. Leah called me the other day. She was putting out a warning to all of the trucking companies in the area, big and small. Her father had been approached and refused to take the contract."

"And it was this company?"

"I think so. I mean, the name is a little different than what she gave, but that's what they'd do, isn't it?"

"Change the name enough that we couldn't connect the two?" Brett looked up as he heard footsteps and Branigan appeared in the doorway, entering as Brett motioned him in. "That's exactly what they would do. Here, Branigan. You can look into this."

Branigan took the paperwork handed him, glancing through it briefly. "I would suggest you not take on this company for deliveries. We came across it actually last night when we were doing some research. Brenden red-flagged it for further investigation. What he had discovered was that the Langs are somehow involved with it."

"It all comes back to them, doesn't it? But who is behind them? None of them had the smarts to think this up." Guenivere was lost in thought as soon as she had spoken, her mind tracing the family and what friends she knew they had.

Branigan read back through the material, slower this time, his pen out to make notes before he looked up at Brett, who had gone back to his own paperwork.

"Brett? I think I know who this is. We've had dealings with someone who talks like this. I need to speak with Barnabas to be sure."

Brett nodded, pointing to the papers. "Take that with you. Now, you two. Off with you. We're closing up for the day." He rose, tidying away his work, and then following the young couple through the office, securing the door after setting the security system. "Don't come in tomorrow, Guenivere. I've closed the office for the day. Mom and I are going to that conference for the weekend. Douglas will handle the men in the warehouse."

"I can come in, Dad." She paused as he shook his head. "Okay, I'll work from home. I'll send Douglas anything that he may need."

The next afternoon, Guenivere wandered the gardens around the building, finally settling down in a seat near the rose garden. She looked around, feeling safe for a moment, but then feeling she was being watched. She rose, spinning around, and running for the building, hearing footsteps behind her that spurred her to run faster, reaching the back door, wrenching it open and then pulling it closed behind her before she ran for the stairs, heading for her own apartment. She heard the door open cautiously behind her and peeked over the railings, seeing the tallest of their kidnappers standing there, searching for her.

She covered her mouth to control her gasp before she sped on silent feet the rest of the way to her apartment, struggling to find the lock and then shutting the door and locking it behind her. She heard movement in the hall and peeked out the peephole, seeing the man trying the doors as he walked along. Her door rattled, even as her hand rested on the lock, as she drew in a deep breath, desperate to control her sobs. She slid to the floor, her head buried on her knees until she could control herself and then rose, determination in her stride and headed for the office.

Will hung up the phone, disturbed by his conversation with Guenivere, and then rose, heading to find Dallas, who was nowhere in the building. He finally sighed, reached for his keys and walked out, heading for the building to talk in person with Guenivere. He knew he should wait for Dallas, but it was too urgent.

Barnabas met him in the lobby, a frown on his face.

"Will? What's this I hear?"

Will nodded. "He followed her into the building and then went along the hallways, trying the doors. She just made it in to her own in time by the sounds of it."

"I don't like that, not one bit. Listen, the guys are gathering tonight for prayer and then to work on this. Brady heard from Emma and she was sending stuff by courier, which I think had just arrived. Can you stay?"

Will shook his head. "I wish I could. Call Dallas. He's been assigned to this case. Give him what you can, unless Emma's already sent it on to him."

"She has. Not as much as before, but she's still working on it, she said. She's put Jace, I think she called him, on it full time."

"Good. Now I need to find Guenivere and have a chat with her, then direct her to Dallas. This is getting old, you know."

Barnabas grinned for a moment as Will walked away before he looked around and saw Branigan standing near him, puzzlement on his face.

"Barnabas? Will is here?"

"He is." Barnabas pointed to the chairs near the one fireplace. "Let's have a seat. Will wants to talk to Guenivere before you do."

"What happened today?" Branigan was torn. He wanted to hear what happened, but he wanted to find his lady and ensure that she was okay.

"Apparently, Guenivere went wandering in the gardens and found the ladies' favourite bench near the rose garden. She says she felt someone watching her and ran for the building, hearing footsteps behind her. It was the tallest of your kidnappers." Barnabas paused, anger growing in him. "He followed her into the building through the back door. He went along the hallways, checking for an unlocked door. She could have disappeared and no one would have known."

Branigan sat back, his face stern and sober, as he mulled over what he had been told. "We can't lock her away. She needs to have some freedom. And no one can be with her all the time." He sighed. "Now, what do we do?"

"We meet tonight and come up with some plans. Hopefully, your lady will be agreeable."

"She might but she is also finding her voice as she brings hope back into her life. Be prepared to have a battle or two over this."

Chapter 19

Branigan looked up that evening, from the paperwork he had been studying, the schematics of the system he had designed for Brett. They were his plans, Joseph had followed them, but somehow, someone had tampered with them. He suspected someone in the company. He rose, heading for Benen and with a quiet word, asked if he would investigate a name for him. Benen looked startled and then nodded.

Branigan stood back, watching his friends, from all over the country, and thought how well God had chosen each one to become part of the Foundation family. He paused to pray for each individual man, knowing some faced danger every day in their employment. He paused as he came to Barnabas, for some reason a heavier burden weighing him down for his friend and employer. Why, he had no idea, he only knew he had to pray for him.

Breck watched Branigan closely. He did that with the men, assessing who needed time away, who needed someone to talk to, who just needed someone to stand with them. This time, Branigan needed that, to have someone just standing with him, not saying a word.

Branigan looked up as Breck's hand rested briefly on his shoulder.

"Branigan, how are you doing in all this? Do you need to talk to someone?"

"Actually, Breck, I'm doing okay. Burnie and I have talked, thanks." He looked around. "A lot of activity going on, isn't there?"

"There is. It seems to get busier each time one of us goes through this." He paused, his eyes on the doorway. "Guenivere is here." His hand stopped Branigan from moving towards her. "Wait. She's here to talk to someone. Let her do that first. She knows where you are."

Branigan sighed. "She does. This is hard, you know. Standing back when I want to make it all better for her. But to move in and take over would do her a disservice. She needs to learn to have that hope in God and that trust, doesn't she's?"

"She does. She has more than any of us realized. She called me after she called Will, demanding to know how she was to stay safe if the monster, as she called him, could get into the building and follow her right to her apartment. She's correct in asking that. Security is working on something but if that door had been locked or she had had to key in a passcode, she would not be standing here today."

"That's what frightens me. We seem no further ahead than we were." He looked up as Will spoke his name. "Will, I thought you had left."

"I was in my car when the coroner called. I spoke with Dallas. He'll be out to go over more of the details, but we have a name on the skeleton Guenivere found." He jumped a bit as a sound came from beside him.

Branigan reached for his lady, drawing her close, his eyes back on Will. "Who was it?"

Guenivere spoke. "It was Jason's father, wasn't it?"

Will nodded. "Your guess from the start was correct, Guenivere. We don't know how he died at this point. There was not a lot of evidence that the team could find. When we catch the men after you, I am sure they'll be able to tell us. Stay as safe as you two can. Guenivere, please do not wander around too much on your own. Each one of these men in here have come to myself and Barnabas, offering to escort you where you need to go. That is, if Branigan is not available." He grinned at the look she shot him. "I'm off. Dallas said he'd be out tomorrow."

Branigan began to shake with suppressed laughter at the look of affront on his lady's face, causing her to turn and glare at him in turn before she broke away and walked over to where Brennen was at work, sitting beside him and drawing him out on what he had found.

Breck had watched with amusement, finally grinning openly as he watched the dialogue between the two.

"You shouldn't have laughed, you know."

Branigan's grin widened. "I know. I am going to have to apologize for that."

"Nope, not apologize. Grovel would be a good way to go."

"And why would Branigan have to grovel?" Brody spoke from Branigan's other side.

"He laughed at something Will said, tried to hide it and got found out."

Brody grinned. "Then I agree. Grovel it is. Listen, I have found some information on Douglas that I think we need to look further at. It could be a plant, but we need to verify it."

"That bad?" Breck questioned.

"I can't tell for sure. Not until I know for sure it's correct. Listen, I'm off. I have to be on the road by three tomorrow morning. Call me if you need me." He walked away, leaving the two men exchanging glances before Branigan spoke.

"I would hate to think it was Douglas."

"Me, too. He's such a part of their family, but as such would be a good plant. We're looking at all the drivers and the warehouse staff as well."

"I am sure you are. I'm off to draw my lady away and grovel. See you later." He walked towards Guenivere, finding her on her feet, heading his way, taking the hand he had outstretched to her.

Once outside the conference room, they walked slowly to the lobby, finding seats on a couch. Branigan's arm drew her close.

"So, how much grovelling are you planning on doing?" She smirked at him until he laughed.

"Let me guess. Brennen spilled the beans."

"He did. He said the other five men have had to do that, and you thought it was amusing. So it was only fair that you had to." She laughed at the remembrance of the look on Brennen's face before she sobered. "What all did Will have to say?"

"Not much, other than what he said." Branigan grew silent, content to have his lady love in his arms, her hands wrapped around his. The silence grew, both not eager to speak.

"Did you know that Fynn asked Brady to marry her?"

Branigan grinned at the remembrance. "I do. Buckley was there, but kept quiet about it until the two had told us. He doesn't let her forget, you know."

"I can see that. He has quite the sense of humour, needed in his job. He has no one he's dating?"

"None of us did. Not until we met the lady we want to spend the rest of our lives with." His voice died away as he groaned to himself. *Did I really go and say that, Lord? I'm ready for the next step, but I am not sure that Guenivere is.*

Guenivere had been listening closely to his words, her mind stilling as she heard the present tense in his sentence, her heart rising in hope. She finally twisted in his arms so she could look in his face, finding him staring across the room, a contrite expression on his face.

"Did you mean that, Branigan?" Her voice was quiet enough he barely heard her words.

He looked down at her. "I did. I just didn't mean to say them. Not yet."

"But why? Don't you know that gives me hope, hope that I will have someone in my life for the rest of it? Lang took that hope away from me for so long, but you have brought it back. You and God."

Branigan studied her face, drinking in her beauty, seeing her heart once more in her eyes.

"I just thought you needed time. Time to learn to live with the hope I see rising in you."

"But don't you see, you're the one who has helped me do that. You didn't stop asking, looking out for me, taking care of me in a way that no one else ever has."

"I don't want gratitude, Guenivere."

"You will have my gratitude but you're correct when you state that you want to spend the rest of my life with me, is that not true?" At his nod, her hands reached for his. "Don't you see? That's my hope, Branigan. My hope that drives me, keeps me going, helps me to trust God more and more. You have helped me to see it wasn't me, wasn't my fault, that I can and must let go of the past and reach for God and trust Him to lead, no matter what I go through."

Chapter 20

Two days later, Branigan stood in the hallway outside of Guenivere's apartment, staring at the open door, the meal he had picked up for them to share dropping to the floor. He reached to touch the door, nodding. He was not seeing anything. The door was open. He walked cautiously in and through the apartment, even checking out the balcony, not finding his love. He spun in a circle, his hand on his head, trying to think of where she would be. She had been adamant that she would be at home. She was working on the contract renewals for some of their clients and was determined to have them done that day.

Blair stopped on his way by, staring down at the bag on the floor before he picked it up, tapping at the door and entering.

"Guenivere? Are you here?" He seemed startled to have Branigan appear at once. "Where's Guenivere?"

"Not here, and she should be. Something is off. She wouldn't have just walked away. Not now."

"No?" Blair's hand drew Branigan from the apartment. "For now, we need to call it in. Come. Sit with me in our apartment. Devaney may know something."

Branigan perked up. "Yes, she might. What are we waiting for?" He headed on a run down the hallway, not waiting for Blair.

Blair dropped his head, shaking it, before he headed for his own home, walking in to find Devaney staring at Branigan, her mouth open.

"No, I haven't seen her today. None of us have. I spoke with her around nine, to see if she wanted to come for lunch, but she said she had contracts that she wanted to get done. Isn't she home?"

"She's not, and the door is wide open. That's not her."

"No, it's not." Devaney spun, reaching for her phone, calling Alice. "Alice? Are you on duty? You are. Good. Listen, Branigan just found Guenivere's door open and no sign of her. He walked through, he said, and then Blair brought him here. No, sorry. Branigan ran for here, Blair following at a slower pace." She made a face at Blair as he shook a finger at her. "Sure. No. We'll be here. Do I need to call it in? Oh, okay, you'll do that? Sure. Come, find us. Branigan?" Her eyes sought the other man, finding him standing, hands on his head, staring at the floor, devastation on his face for a moment. "No, we'll make sure he stays put. Thank you."

Devaney set her phone down, her eyes on Branigan before she glanced at Blair and nodded at the question on his face. She approached Branigan, a hand on his arm bringing him back from wherever it was he had wandered off to.

"Alice is working tonight. She'll come out. She said she'd bring a team with her to search the apartment."

"Thank you." He looked up as Blair handed him a mug of coffee and then with a sigh, shoved him down into a chair. "Where do we search, Blair?"

"For now, we don't. We let Alice and her crew work it through. Then, we spread out." Blair sat, laying his phone on the table. "I sent out a group text. The guys will meet in the conference room. The ladies will meet here. It's our standard plan."

Branigan nodded. "I know. We decided we needed that after you and Devaney. It just doesn't make it any easier, you know."

"No, it doesn't but it helps to have them involved. Buckley responded that he'd make his way here. He was driving back home from that funeral two hours away. He thought he'd be here in about thirty minutes."

"Then, he won't have eaten." Devaney was on her feet, her hand on the fridge door, before her head turned, watching her friend before looking at Blair, who simply shook his head once more.

"Branigan, do you want anything to eat?" Devaney had to ask twice to raise his head up from the folded arms he had laid it on. He looks tired, she thought, tired and worn out. The accident took from his strength. Worrying about Guenivere does not help.

Branigan took a moment to process what she had asked. "No, I don't think so. Just coffee is fine." He didn't look up, didn't see the sandwich that she set in front of him, reaching automatically for it after Blair had prayed.

Blair and Devaney shook their heads at one another. He's working on autopilot, Blair thought. That is not good. He rose as he heard a quiet tap at the door and stepped outside, not surprised to find both Will and Dallas there.

"Branigan?" Will's voice held concern, concern for Branigan as Guenivere's boyfriend but also concern for a friend.

"He's inside. We managed to get him to eat, but he's not really aware of what he is doing." He looked down the hall past them. "What have you found?"

"They've just gotten started." Dallas turned for a moment. "Do you know who she may have talked to today?"

"Devaney said they spoke around nine. I can't say if she's talked to anyone else. If her phone is there, that should show you."

"It is, but it is password secured." Dallas nodded at the door. "Would Branigan know her password?"

Blair nodded. "Try his first or last name. That might work. Or the town in PEI that he's from."

Dallas thanked him and walked back down the hall. Will stood for a moment, lost in thought. "I need to speak with Branigan, but I have to let him speak to Dallas first. Where can we talk, Blair?"

"Head for the conference room. Most of the guys will be there. The ladies will be heading our way as is Buckley, when he gets in." He watched as Alice approached and quietly asked Will to come with her.

Chapter 21

His arm around Lena, Brett began to shake his head as he stared at Will, not believing what he had to say.

"She can't have disappeared. I talked to her about two, going over some details on one of the contracts. She had that one and one other to finish, she said."

"As I said, her door was wide open when Branigan arrived there tonight. We have searched her apartment and are in the process of searching the building and then the surrounding buildings. We'll start a search of the grounds in the morning, bringing in the K-9 units."

"But how, Will? How could she just disappear? She wouldn't have walked out on her own, not knowing that Branigan would be there. She was looking forward to their meal together. They did that every night and then went for walks." Lena's hand covered her mouth for a moment. "I talked to her before work started, and she didn't seem any different than she had."

Will nodded. "Thanks, Brett. Lena. I'm heading back to the Foundation. If you two want to come, Barnabas said he'd make arrangements for you." He paused, a thought crossing his mind. "Where is Douglas?"

"Douglas? Haven't you heard? He was walking across a street down town over the lunch hour and was hit. The car disappeared."

Will paused, a thought crossing his mind. "I'll look into that. I'm on my way back. I just wanted to speak with Douglas, to see if he had thought of anything else that he could remember."

"We talked this morning, Will. He was waiting for me when I got there. He's so distraught. That could be why he didn't see the car. He and his wife, as you know, lost their daughter at age two. Guenivere sort of helped to fill the emptiness for them."

"I remember, and I understand." Will walked away, heading for his vehicle, deep in thought. He slid behind the wheel, but didn't drive off. Something kept his there, his eyes searching through darkness before he was out of his car, running towards the dark form he could see, tackling the younger man and taking him to the ground, before he slapped handcuffs on him. He stood, towering over the man, the man's wallet in his hand, before he reached for his phone and called it in.

Will reached down and yanked the man to his feet, a little rougher than he normally would have.

"Okay, John Jones. Up you go. I have a ride coming for you, and a nice detective to speak with you. I want to know why you were sneaking up on this house. You're not from this neighbourhood, so it really makes me suspicious of your motives."

Dallas sat back, staring at Will. "You found him where?"

"At Brett's. I had stopped by there and something wouldn't let me leave. I found him sneaking up on the house. He had a knapsack with him. I'll leave it for you to talk to him. I'm heading back out."

Dallas stood, following Will down the hallway. "No word?'

Will shook his head. "Not a word. No ransom demand. No note asking for Branigan or Brett to do something." He pulled out his phone, checking the number. "Let me get this and then if we need to talk, come find me. If not, you know where I'll be. I hope we can at least keep the media down to a dull roar."

Dallas gave a slow nod of his head. "It's funny. They would usually be all over this, but Jim, the news editor from the local station, called. They have all agreed to keep it low key and as quiet as they can. The Foundation has done too much good in our community, he said, for them to do them any harm."

"That's a relief. If they keep it low key, then it can be controlled." He walked away, Dallas watching him before he turned, heading for one of the interrogation rooms and John Jones.

Branigan stirred as he felt a hand on his shoulder and looked up from the chair he had slumped down into, not wanting to leave the conference room and the work that was going on there. He started to rise, meeting Brett's eyes and then kept his seat. Brett sat next to him, his face buried in his hands for a moment.

"Brett?" Branigan's voice was quiet, just loud enough that Brett heard him. "Have you heard anything?"

"No." Brett looked up, his chin resting on his hand, the other hand rubbing at the table. "Will stopped by. As he was leaving, he tackled someone sneaking towards our house. I haven't heard yet why or who."

Branigan shook his head. "I wish I knew where to look for Guenivere. I talked to her about three, just to find out what she wanted for her meal. She sounded fine, just like herself."

"And you got here, what about five or so?"

"That's correct." Branigan looked up to find Dallas sliding into a chair at the table, his notepad and pen out. "Dallas?"

Dallas shook his head even as he gave a somber smile. "Just a few questions, Branigan. Brett. I need to clarify something." He turned to Brett. "You said Guenivere was working on contacts?"

Brett nodded. "She was. We have some new clients that we had to have the contracts ready for, and a couple whose contracts were expiring. She always has everything ready well ahead of time, says we can't run a fair or reliable business if we don't." He looked down at his folded hands. "She had emailed me all of them by late this afternoon. I can check the timing of that for you, but when I checked around five, they were waiting for me."

Branigan nodded. "I received a text message around four, just to say she had them done and had some other work waiting." He paused, a thought crossing his mind. "Did she send that text though? How do we know for sure?"

"We don't, not until we find her and can ask her." Dallas looked down at his notes. "I think that's all for now. I will have other questions as we go along." He looked up, assessing the two men he was with. "We'll find her for you. That's a promise."

Chapter 22

A day passed by without any word, then another and another until two weeks went along and the calendar flipped to a new page. Branigan grew thin and white, the shadows under his eyes creeping darker and darker. He slept little, wandering the fields and forest around the building, searching through their town, moving to other towns and villages in the area. To no avail. He could not find her, no matter how he looked.

Brett and Lena were almost constant companions of the men and ladies of the building, helping to research, trying their best to stay positive but failing. Brett had privately told Barnabas that he had taken Lena to their physician the day before after he came home and found her collapsed on the floor, unconscious. Branigan had spent time with them, and with Douglas. He had searched around the property Brett had his business on to no avail as well. Guenivere had simply disappeared.

His friends were spending every moment they could helping to search, to research, to talk to people. Buckley and Brendon had headed to the streets of the town, talking to everyone and anyone they could. The Foundation board had approached Brett and offered to put up a reward, if it came to that. He had looked at his fellow members and with tears in his ears and broken words, had thanked them.

Brennen stood for a moment, those two weeks later, his eyes on Branigan as he sat in the lobby, a mug of tea at his side on the table. He had stopped drinking coffee, just why, he couldn't tell them. He approached his friend, dropping into a chair near him, waiting, needing to talk to him, but unsure of how to do just that.

"Brennen? You have news?" Branigan rubbed at his gritty, red eyes.

"I do. I'm just not sure if it's accurate or not. Someone approached me today, one of the down and outers that Buckley ministers to. He handed me a paper and then took off. On it was an address. I looked it up. It's in Ennis' town."

"We've searched there, haven't we, without finding anything?"

"We have, but somehow, this is different. I want to go take a look, without alerting anyone. I think there's a leak somewhere in the investigation, but I can't prove it."

Branigan sat up, an alert look on his face. "I know. It's like someone is watching us, knowing what we know, and then staying one or two steps ahead of us." He looked down. "I trust Will, Dallas and Alice but someone else is involved."

"I know. I'm trying to determine who. Emma's been in touch. She has some names to run, she said, something she picked up in her investigation. She'll talk to Barnabas and Will, she said, when she has more information."

"She does? Good." Branigan turned his mug around and around on the counter. "Brennen, are you heading over to Ennis' town?"

"I am. Listen. I talked to her cousin, Eric. He and his captain are willing to help, on their own time. I told him to talk to Barnabas, see where they would fit the best."

"That's good." Branigan gave a huge, down to his toes, sigh as he laid his head back on the couch, slouching down once more. "I want her home, Brennen." His phone vibrated against his side and he ignored it, finally pulling it out with a muttered comment when it kept vibrating. He squinted at it, not recognizing the number, before he answered.

"Hello? Hello? Is someone there?" He waited, hearing soft rustling in the background. "Who's there?"

"Branigan?" The voice was ever so faint, but ever so dear to his heart. "Branigan? Come get me. Please? I need you to come get me."

"Guenivere? Oh, my love, where are you?" He was on his feet, heading for the door, Brennen beside him, pointing to his own truck. "Keep talking to me. We're coming, but I need to know where you are."

"It's dark, Branigan. It's dark. I can see the sky above me, but I can't climb up. Please, Branigan? Come get me?" Her voice died away, but Branigan could hear the soft whisper of her breathing, and then her soft sobs. It tore at his heart, hearing her but not being able to comfort her.

Brennen's phone was in his hand, his voice quiet as he listened to Branigan, asking to be put through to either Dallas or Will.

"Dallas? Listen. You have Branigan's phone number. Is it possible for you to trace it?" He listened. "I know. It's a long shot, but he's on his phone right now with Guenivere. She can't tell us where she is but it sounds as if she may be underground or down in a hole or well." He listened, his eyes shooting to Branigan. "Over there? Sure. I'll head that way." His phone hit the cup holder in the console, as he drove away rapidly, halting briefly as he met Brady and Bradon coming back in. He could see Bradon's dog, Kade, in the back seat, his chin on Bradon's shoulder.

"Brady. Follow me. Do you have your emergency kit with you?"

"Always." Brady ducked his head to stare through the window at Branigan, watching as his friend spoke quietly on the phone. "What's up?"

"Guenivere. Branigan's on the phone with her. She called, asking him to come find her."

"What?" Bradon leaned over the console to look at Brennen. "How?"

"We are not sure. It is just so bizarre. I asked Dallas to try and trace her call, but he wasn't sure if he could. She seems to be underground or in a hole or something."

"The old mill. There's an abandoned well near there." Bradon shared a look with Brady. "Let's try there. It all seems to come back to that property. Did we ever research that?”

“Burnie muttered something yesterday about it. I think he was.” Brennen drove off as quickly as he could, Brady spinning his wheel to turn his truck and follow.

“Where’s Doc today?” Bradon’s voice broke through the silence in the cab.

“At home. Call him. We may need him.”

Bradon was already dialling Doc, speaking rapidly, hearing the sound of surprise in Doc’s voice. He pocketed his phone. “He said he’d grab some supplies from the infirmary, including the backboard and collar.”

“I don’t like the thought of that, but we may well need them.”

The trucks parked, the men shot out of them, Kade milling around before he caught a scent and tugged at his leash, pulling Bradon with him.

“Has he picked up something?” Brady shouldered his bag and ran after them, Brennen and Branigan following on his heels.

“He’s picked up something. He has that ability to learn the scent of every one of us. Guenivere spent time with us, and Kade had taken to her. I pray that’s who he’s picking up.”

Fifteen minutes later, they slid to a halt, Kade on his belly, head hanging over a hole in the ground, a soft woof echoing back. Bradon reached for the large flashlight he was handed and carefully knelt, aiming the beam downwards. His heart caught for a moment, seeing that the hole was at least fifteen or more feet deep before the light flashed across something. He moved the beam back and a sudden yell from him startled the three men.

"Bradon?" Branigan hardly dared to breathe.

"She's there, Branigan. Kade found her. Now to get down to her." He stood, his hand reaching to grip his friend's shoulder. "I can't see if she's hurt, it's deep enough."

Branigan nodded, reaching for the harness Brady had pulled from his pack. "I'm going down, Brady. I have to."

Brady hesitated, knowing that he should be the one, that if Guenivere was hurt, he had to be the one to bring her up but he didn't have the heart to say no.

"Okay, you go down. Let me know how she is. If I have to, I pull you back up and go down myself."

Branigan stared at him, his hand on the harness that Brady had not released. "That's fine. Just let me go."

Bradon stopped their conversation with a simple statement. "First, we pray. We need to do that, guys."

Branigan hesitated when they were finished, torn between wanting to go down to Guenivere but knowing that he was not the best person. He turned to Brady, finding his friend watching him intently. He stared down at the harness he held in his hand before he thrust it back at Brady.

"You go. You have the training and are used to this. I don't. God help me, I don't want to hurt her, not if I can help it."

Brady's hand was out to grasp the harness, hearing the quiet murmurs of agreement from the other two. "You're sure?"

Branigan gave a quick nod. "I am. Go, before I change my mind."

Brady was into the harness, the rope attached and then tied off on a nearby tree. They had to call Kade back from the edge, Bradon gripping his leash shortly. He was not moving, his whole body seemed to say, not when a friend was down there. He needed to help, his quiet woof said.

Brady dropped to the edge of the hole before his body twisted and he began to feel his way down, hearing bits of dirt and debris falling. The others stayed away from the edge, not wanting to cave it in. Branigan's gloved hands helped to feed the rope, hearing Brady call that he was on the bottom.

Their arrival had disturbed the quietness of the morning, sending the creatures and birds to hiding before they once more came out, their eyes on the men, before they decided that they meant them no harm. The three men had their focus on the rope and Brady, not seeing the man who had approached and then withdrawn to the shadows of the nearby trees, curses coming in from him. He felt for his phone, not finding it. He cursed once more as his eyes sought out Branigan, blaming him for the loss. He had no idea where it was but if they were here, how did they find her? She wasn't to be found. Not yet. Maybe not ever.

Chapter 23

Doc approached the three men, Brennen turning as he heard him and walking towards him in a rapid manner.

"Doc?" Brennen reached for the backboard. "We found her. Brady's down in the well with her."

"He is? I thought Branigan would have been."

"He wanted to, but he stopped himself, telling Brady he didn't have the training that Brady had. It was very hard on him to stop himself."

Doc looked behind him. "Barnabas was rounding up the rest of the men, meeting in the conference room. I told him we would call once we knew something." Doc's phone was in his hand. "Barnabas? Good news." A relieved smile broke across Doc's face. "Brennen says they found her. Brady's with her. What's that? No. We don't know much yet. I think Dallas is on the way. Buckley said he would call him, when I saw him just as I was leaving. Good. We'll let you know once we have more information."

His phone pocketed, Doc looked past Brennen. "Branigan?"

"He's relieved, Doc, but there is that uncertainty right now. We don't know if she's hurt or how bad, or even how she got in there."

"No, we don't. Here's Dallas and his team."

Dallas approached cautiously, hope rising but he refused to let it rise all the way until he was sure.

"Brennen? Is she here? I tried to trace her call but couldn't."

"She is, Dallas. I was telling Doc that Brady is down with her."

They turned, walking rapidly back towards the well, seeing Bradon leaning cautiously over, his hand gripped in Branigan's to keep his balance. He looked up and then spoke rapidly to Brady.

"Doc? Brady wants the backboard and collar sent down. He doesn't think she has any injury but he's not wanting to take any chances."

"Send it down. Dallas, are paramedics on the way?"

"They are. I sent in a call once you confirmed she was here. They're ten minutes out."

Bradon looked around, relief on his face to see Doc. Branigan pulled him back from the edge and turned as well, surprise on his face to see Dallas and Doc both.

"Doc? Dallas?"

"We're here, Branigan. How be you move back for now? The paramedics were right behind me and I think they were sending firefighters as well just in case they were needed in the extraction." Dallas' hand on his arm kept Branigan in place before he moved back. "What can you tell me? Brennen said you had a call."

"I did, Dallas. She called me. I wasn't going to answer as I didn't know the number. She asked me to come and find her, that it was dark where she was." Branigan squinted up at the sky, watching as twilight was moving in. "We need to call Brett and Lena."

"Alice is taking care of that. She'll have them taken to the hospital for now." Dallas looked around, watching close before he was off on the run, heading for the trees, the officer approaching them heading his way instead.

The men turned, a frown on each other of their faces, before they exchanged glances and then headed for the well.

Brady stood at the bottom, looking up with relief as he heard Doc's voice.

"Doc? You're here. Backboard and collar?"

"On the way down. How is she?"

"She's been talking. She is angry, I can tell you that much. I need help down here but there is not enough room. Let me see what I can do."

They could hear Brady's voice quietly speaking to Guenivere and on occasion, what they hoped was her voice responding. Finally, a tug came on the rope attached to the backboard.

"I'm ready to come up. What I need is to be pulled up at the same time as Guenivere, that way I can help to stabilize her a bit."

"Will do. We're ready." Brennen looked around at the men gathered, his friends, Doc, and the waiting paramedics as well as the crime scene team Dallas had brought with him. We have almost too many volunteers, he thought.

Branigan's breath came out in a rush as Guenivere appeared at the top of the well and hands reached out for the backboard she was strapped to and then for Brady who was on his knees beside her almost before she was on the ground, Doc on the other side, the two paramedics who had been summoned with them. He waited, edging closer, his eyes on his beloved's face.

Doc looked up, and gave a grim smile. "She's alive, Branigan. How serious she is, I can't tell you yet. We need to get her to the hospital. Ready, fellows?"

Willing hands reached to raise her as the men lifted her and then turned to walk away. Guenivere roused, her eyes shooting around in fear, before she spied Branigan, a hand raising for him to grasp. He walked beside her, almost tripping over his own feet, Brennen's hand on his shoulder steadying him.

Doc followed, in quiet conversation with Brady, before he looked up. Surprise overcame him as he saw Dallas and the officer returning with their prisoner. A closer look at the man drew a startled exclamation from Doc.

"Trevor Lang?"

"It is, Doc. He was in the woods waiting. In fact, it was his cell phone that Guenivere used. I did find out that much." Dallas looked with almost anger on the man. "He has a lot to say."

“I want my lawyer.” Lang’s mouth snapped shut and he refused to say another word, not even when he was shoved forward to walk back towards the road.

Chapter 24

Brett and Lena almost ran into the Emergency Department, looking for someone, anyone, who could tell them how Guenivere. Will had appeared at their doorway, Brett having come home early, just to be with Lena. She was grieving, he knew, certain that they would never see their daughter again. They had looked at Will in shock, Lena's hand going to her mouth, Brett's arms around her before Will hurried them out to and to his car, speeding away with an escort, hoping to arrive at the same time the ambulance did with Guenivere.

Branigan spun as he felt a hand on his back, Lena reaching to hug him, holding on tighter and longer than she normally would, stepping back only when Brett nudged her to, so he could hug Branigan. He knew, not so much from what his daughter had said but what she hadn't said, that Branigan meant the world to her and would be part of their family at some point.

Will directed them to seats out of the way, a wall of men standing in the way to prevent onlookers from gawking at them, and that would happen, he knew. Brett sank into a chair, suddenly weary, before he looked up at Branigan.

"Branigan? What happened? Will said she called you. How? She didn't have her phone."

"She did. I'm not sure how she got ahold of one but she called. I can't tell you how I felt when I realized it was her and she was alive. Brennen spoke with Dallas who mentioned the well near the mill. We tracked her there, thanks to Kade, and the rest, I guess, is really all that matters. Brady went down, brought her up. Doc's with her right now."

Branigan's head drooped, the sudden release of the tension he had been under drawing all his strength at that moment as a huge wave of fatigue washed over him. He heard a faint call before the world darkened. He roused to find a paramedic crouching down in front of him, Brady's partner in fact.

"Branigan? You okay, man? You almost face planted on the floor."

"I guess. It's the relief."

"That would do it." Patrick shared a look with Will before he checked Branigan's vitals. "You seem alright now. I would suggest something sweet." He held up a hand at the face Branigan pulled. "You need it. Your blood pressure likely dropped and I am sure your blood sugar has as well. You haven't been eating, now have you?" As Branigan shook his head, the paramedic reached for the bottle of juice, uncapped it, and shoved it into his hand. "Drink. I'll go see what I can find out for you. Brady was through but he said he'd stay with your lady as long as they would let him. Doc as well."

Branigan nodded, shame filling him for his reaction at that point. He felt Lena's arm around him, a mother's arm that he could not remember having felt in his life, he thought, and appreciated that his lady's mother was taking him in. He looked up finally as he heard footsteps and then was on his feet walking towards Brady, an unspoken question on his lips.

Brady pointed to the outside doors, steering Branigan that way. Patrick had found him, had told him Branigan needed some air, and Doc had shooed him away, stating he would stay with Guenivere until she had been assessed. They wouldn't kick him out, he declared, not out of the department he worked in.

Branigan paced away from Brady, who stood, feet planted near the door, watching and assessing his friend. He turned back, paused, and then approached.

"Brady?"

"She's dehydrated for one thing, Branigan. Scrapes. Bruises. They'll do X-rays to look for broken bones."

"Thank you." Branigan's head dropped back as he stared up at the sky, dark now, the moon and stars hiding intermittently behind the scudding clouds, driven by the wind that was picking up. "Did she say anything?

Brady groaned to himself, knowing that Branigan just had to ask that, now didn't he, Lord? How do I answer when I still have to give my statement? This is one time, Lord, I would really appreciate You speaking for me.

"Not a whole lot, Branigan. She didn't seem to understand where she was, being some that disoriented. She did ask about you."

"I don't care about me. Is she okay, that's all I want to know."

"She should be. Brett and Lena will go back but I know you'll be able to. Doc will make sure of that."

Branigan nodded. "Did I hear that Dallas had arrested someone?"

"That's what Doc said. I didn't see him, so I can't say for sure. He'll be around at some point, likely." He turned as he heard the door swish open behind him and Brett appeared.

"Brett?" Branigan's voice held hope?"

"Guenivere is in X-ray right now. We were able to just have a moment or two with her. Doc said he'll get you back when she's in a room." Brett paused, exhaustion draining him. "She's okay, Branigan. They don't think any broken bones or a concussion. Just dehydration." He looked around before he looked at Branigan. "I just don't understand the phone."

"Whoever it was likely dropped it. I'm sure he's missing it by now." Branigan gave a sudden grin. "Is this one of those times Buckley would call a God moment?"

The other two men laughed for a moment before a voice spoke beside them.

"That I would, and yes, it was." Buckley stood there, exhaustion evident in his face. He had not slept much, spending the time he was unable to in prayer for his friends. "This is getting old, guys. I thought we were told no more adventures."

"That we were, but we just don't seem to be able to avoid them." Branigan paced away, his eyes on a car that was hovering on the street.

The driver saw Branigan coming and sped away, leaving a dark streak of rubber on the pavement. Branigan stood, his eyes narrowed, unable to get a really good description of the car or driver, and certainly not the license plate number.

Chapter 25

A day later, Branigan perched on the arm of the couch in Guenivere's living room, watching as she paced, albeit slowly. She had adamantly refused to go home, not saying why, but he had read the fear she had tried to hide from everyone. She's afraid, isn't she, Lord? Afraid to bring the men to her family. But that's too late. It's already happened. When they told her, that brought it home to the Danbys.

"Sweetheart? Don't you think you should sit?" He rose, stepping into her path and stopping her with his hands on her upper arms before he pulled her into a hug. She stiffened and tried to pull away, before she relaxed against him, her arms coming around to hug him back.

"I'm so afraid, Branigan. So deeply afraid."

"I know you are. We need to talk about what happened and why you're afraid." He turned her to the couch, sitting and drawing her down with him, an arm wrapped around her to hold her tight to him. "What did he threaten you with?"

She shook her head. "It wasn't a him. It was a woman. I know the voice but I can't think of who it was." Her head tilted to look up at him. "I never told you last night what happened. Dallas was there so late to get my statement and then they gave me something to sleep. I hated that."

"I know." His fingers twisted at the ring he had placed on her finger earlier that day, stating simply that he loved her dearly and when she had been gone he didn't want to live. Would she be his? She had simply nodded, exhaustion taking her voice.

"I need to talk. There are some things I couldn't tell Dallas. I have to at some point, but I needed to talk to you first." She stared up at him, distraught, before he leaned over and kissed her.

"Talk to me, my love. Tell me what happened. I came home that afternoon, with our supper, found your door open and you gone."

Guenivere nodded. "It was. I still don't understand how they got in the building." She frowned for a moment. "They must have come in through the back. That's how they took me out." She looked horrified. "Are the security guys in on it?"

"No. That was Barnabas' first thought but they weren't. Go on."

Guenivere stared ahead at the far wall, gathering her thoughts.

"Okay, so. I was working on those contracts and had just finished them. I think it was just before four. I had walked to the kitchen to make another cup of tea or something like that, I wasn't sure what I actually wanted. I didn't hear the door open. Just felt that I wasn't alone. I didn't get a chance to look around. They slapped a cloth of some kind over my mouth. I struggled to get away, but couldn't escape the hands holding me. I must have passed out at that point, because the next thing I know I'm waking up in a room somewhere. Where I have no idea. It was really rough and damp and cold. I had a blanket to lie on and one to cover me. I was really dizzy when I stood up and reached for a bottle of water. I am not sure now that I should have but I had to have something to drink. My mouth was so dry.

"I was alone I think for about a day, when Trevor Lang appeared. He didn't say anything, just stood and watched me, waiting for something. There was another door in the room, behind me. I heard it open and I know it was a woman's footsteps I heard. He just watched her and then watched me. A paper was dropped on the table near me and then she left. He backed away and locked the door behind him.

"I waited, before I reached for the paper. It had a list of demands, one of which was that I was to provide access to our work computers and to both the office and the warehouse. I can't do that.

"This went on for a couple of weeks. That bottle of water was all I had that first day, a new one given to me each day, with little food provided. The third day or so, he grabbed me by the arm and shoved me out of the room into the sunlight. I couldn't see where I was. Shoved into a car, he tied my hands and then drove away and around for quite a while. Finally, he pulled me from the car, pushed me through the field until we came to that abandoned well. I fought him, trying to get away. It was no use. He wrapped a rope around me, tied it and then shoved me over the edge of the well. I screamed, cried for him not to, but he lowered me to the bottom. I was spinning at the speed he did that, banging into the wall, trying to fend it away and to protect myself. I know I was asking God for help, to stop him. He didn't, Branigan. He just didn't.

"I don't remember much, other than waking up yesterday I guess it was, and looking up, knowing there was no way I could get out of there on my own. I finally was able to untie the rope and stand, leaning on the wall. I saw something on the ground and reached for it, falling back down. It was a phone, Branigan. All I could think of was would I be able to open it and would I be able to make a call. You don't know the relief I felt when I heard your voice."

Guenivere stopped, her emotions and strength draining away, her head slipping down on his shoulder as he tightened his arms around her. Branigan rested his chin on her head, watching as Brett and Lena had entered and found seats, horrified at what they were hearing.

She slept, Branigan not moving, not willing to wake her. An hour passed and he took with thanks the plate of food and mug of coffee that Lena set down beside him. He didn't know if he could eat, but he would try.

Brett had excused himself and walked away, his phone out to talk with Dallas. His face was grim when he returned, simply shaking his head at Branigan before he glanced at Lena. They would talk, he seemed to be saying but not right then.

Guenivere had finally awakened, stumbled to her feet and to her bedroom. Lena had followed, waiting until her daughter had showered, changed into warm pyjamas although the night was warm, and crawled into bed. She stood, her heart sorrowing for her, raising a prayer for healing. She could feel anger in her and knew she shouldn't but at the moment she could feel nothing else. God would understand, she thought, and took her anger to Him.

Brett had walked with Branigan back to the younger man's apartment, few words between them, before he prayed with him, a hand on his shoulder and then watched as Branigan had locked himself away inside. He paused, not sure where he wanted to be, turning to find Buckley and Brody waiting for him, drawing him down to the chapel in the building, where the other men and the ladies were waiting. They knew it would only get worse for the couple and they had no choice but to bathe them in prayer.

Chapter 26

A few days later, Branigan looked up from his desk in the building before rising and walking towards the door, listening carefully before he opened it to peek out. He frowned. The two men he could see wandering down the hallway did not belong to the building's family and he didn't think they were here for an appointment. That's not how the offices worked. He slipped out of his door, quietly locking it behind him, and walked rapidly to the security desk, finding two of the guards there. A few words and the men were heading for the corridor Branigan had just exited. He heard raised voices before the security officers were back, the two men in handcuffs.

Barnabas stood for a moment, watching with a frown on his face as the men were shoved into the police cruisers and one officer approached him.

"Bob?"

"Branigan found them wandering in the building and your security guys nabbed them. They're known to us. They weren't here for the good of any of you."

"I surmised that. Let me know what transpires with them." Barnabas walked away, finding Branigan waiting for him. "Anything to add?"

Branigan shook his voice. "I just don't get it. How are they getting in? They didn't come in from the front."

"No. They would have been stopped, that's a given." Barnabas walked rapidly towards the back door, pausing at one of the empty suites. He studied the door. "This is how, I have no doubt. This door lock has been tampered with. New locks on it and inside I suspect will be in order. I'll let Dallas know so he can look into it before I make any changes here."

Branigan felt a hand touching his back, and turned. Guenivere stood there, a frown on her face.

"Were they here again?" At their nod, she sighed. "Then I guess we need to talk some more. I have had some interesting emails coming to my personal box. I have no idea how they got it."

Branigan stared at her and then at Barnabas, who was already pointing back towards the conference room. "In there. The guys are working, all of them I think."

She nodded and then disappeared down the hall. They heard the door close behind her before Barnabas spoke.

"How did they get that?"

"That's what I don't understand. No one should have it. Unless." Branigan groaned. "The church directory? We have our emails in that. Anyone could pick up an extra from the desk in the foyer."

"That they could. Buckley will see that they are removed right away."

The men who had gathered listened intently as Guenivere explained what she had, handing out copies of the emails. Brennen and Brendon took theirs, putting their heads together for a moment, before looking around and then heading out. Brennen had mentioned quietly that something about the whole thing puzzled him and he needed to do some research in town.

Guenivere finally stood and stretched. She had gotten nowhere, she thought, looking around at the men. She was beginning to get to know them and their personalities as well as some of their likes and dislikes. She named them: Baird, Benen, Blair, Bradon, Brady, Branigan, Brandon, Brendon, Brennen, Brody, Buckley, Burnie, Breck, and of course, Barnabas. Baird's brother-in-law, Darby, was there as was Brady's brother-in-law, Farr, and Farr's cousin, Eric. Dallas had dropped in to get their statements and just stayed. Doc had wandered in and out, ostensibly to see what he could do to help, but she found him watching her and then watching Branigan.

She turned as her phone vibrated, pulling it out, and then frowning at the number. It was not one she knew and let it go to voice mail. Only it never did. That was strange, she thought. It should have gone to voice mail and it didn't. She dropped it on the table and stared at it.

Branigan had looked up at that point, and rose to approach her.

"Something wrong with your phone?"

"I think. It should have gone to voice mail, only it hasn't." She looked up, fear on her face. "Did they tamper with it? But this is a new phone. Dallas has my old one."

Branigan reached for it, scrolling through programs before he stopped. "Here. Someone has downloaded something on it. I would hazard a guess it was when it was bought for you. Let Dallas have it and the details where you got it."

Guenivere simply shuddered and walked away, leaving Branigan staring between her and her phone, a puzzled look on his face. He searched through her phone, finding other programs that should never have been on it. He sighed. It was not getting any easier, now was it? Lord, please? We need this to end, but it doesn't seem as if it will any time soon.

Dallas had approached and Branigan handed him the phone, quietly letting him know what he had found. He had changed the password on it as well, letting Dallas have that. Dallas just shook his head.

"What is it with you guys? You just can't find your ladies in the normal way? You have to dash into danger for them?" He was grumbling in a lighthearted way to try and relieve the tension Branigan was under, but he wasn't even sure that it would work.

Branigan had shaken his head and walked away, heading for the outdoors. He needed some air and some alone time. He paced, his head tilted up to the sky, watching the flickering lights from a plane overhead and then just the twinkling of the stars. The night sounds soothed his mind and heart, bringing a peace as he communed with his Lord.

He turned, not seeing the man who had appeared, not until an iron fist connected with his jaw, sending him flying backwards and down to the ground, to lie still, flat on his back, his arms askew above his head. The man looked around and then lifted Branigan up and over his shoulder, disappearing into the darkness with him.

Benen and Blair walked slowly towards the gym building, needing to wear off some energy, they had declared. They had paused at a sound, looked at each other and shrugged, and continued on their way. Neither saw the man or Branigan disappearing.

Chapter 27

An hour after Branigan had disappeared from the room, Guenivere looked up, needing to ask him something, frowning as she didn't see him. She rose, heading for the door, to be stopped in her tracks by Buckley, who had just entered.

"Buckley? Was Branigan out there?"

Buckley stopped on his way by, searching her face. "No, I didn't see him. I came in from the back, so if he's out front, I wouldn't have. Why? Lose him?" He grinned as she shook a finger at him.

"No. At least, I don't think so. He was here and now he's not. The last I saw him, he was talking with Dallas about my phone. And by the way, those directories in the church foyer? They need to go. We think someone used them to get my email address. The emails I received were not pretty."

Buckley frowned harder. "That's odd. I removed them a month ago, just because of something like this. So, either it was done before then."

Guenivere paled. "Or it's someone in the church or who has access to someone's."

"That's what I think. Now, let's see if we can find your beau."

"Beau?" She laughed as she headed through the door and to the lobby. "Who talks like that?"

"Your mother and father. That's what they call him."

"They do not!" She spun, laughter on her face, not realizing that was the aim of Buckley's teasing. "They don't!"

"On the contrary, they do. Don't you know that?" Buckley stopped, his head turning as he searched the lobby. "Nope. No Branigan. Where is he hiding? And why would he be hiding? You two have a disagreement?"

Guenivere continued to laugh as she headed for the outside. "No, we did not. He took my phone, talked to Dallas, and then I was involved in what I was looking up. Do you know how many Langs there are in the area?"

"No, but I gather you could tell me." Buckley's hand on her arm stopped her forward motion. "Wait for me. We walk together, Guenivere, please."

She paled at his words. "Of course. I'm sorry. I didn't think."

"And that could spell danger or death for you, just keep that in mind." Buckley peered through the darkness. "His truck is still here. I see lights in the gym. Do you suppose?"

"I guess we could check it out, but I don't see that he would be." Guenivere walked forward, step in step with Buckley, before her eyes dropped to the ground and she froze, not able to move.

Buckley walked forward a few feet, then paused, realizing Guenivere was not with him. He turned, his mouth open to tease when he saw her bend over and pick up something from the ground, giving a low cry as she did so. He was back beside her as quickly as he could move

Guenivere looked up, stalling the question that had risen to his lips. "Branigan's phone. He wouldn't have dropped it and not picked it up." Her face paled. "They've taken him, haven't they?"

Buckley's hand was under her arm as he turned her and rushed her back to the building and into the conference room, the violence of how he shoved the door open stopping all activity and causing some of the men to rise in response.

"Buckley? You flew in here for what reason?" Breck approached.

Buckley held out the phone. "Branigan's. We found it on the ground outside. Only there was no Branigan with it."

Breck paused as he reached for it, his eyes on Guenivere, seeing the terror her own eyes held, even as she tried to control her emotions. "Branigan? He's not out there?"

"No. We were looking for him and couldn't find him in the building. We had headed for the gym when Guenivere found this."

"Not another one." Breck spun, his eyes on the men who had stood and were standing behind him. "Fan out, guys. Search the area. See what you can find. Burnie, call it in."

Will stood an hour later, his hand resting on the lobby door, his head bent as he listened to Alice.

"No sign of him?"

"None. We'll need to come back at first light but there doesn't seem to be much disturbance where they found his phone. He's disappeared just like Guenivere did. How do these guys do it?"

"I have no idea. Patrol headed for the mill?"

"They did. They've searched and found nothing. There has to be another building connected to them."

Will held up a finger as his phone chimed and he pulled it out to check a text. "Emma. She's couriering some information on to Dallas. She seems to think she's found something but doesn't want to put it out there on a phone or email."

"It must be big then."

"I would think so. Listen, you're staying here for now. There are two cruisers around as well. I'm heading back into the office. Call if there's any change." He walked away, leaving her staring after him before she turned, a finger tapping at her lips as she thought through what she knew and the buildings in the immediate area. Where is he, Lord? Can You direct us to him? I don't know that Guenivere can take much more. I look at her tonight and see the hope she had found fading. I don't like that.

Chapter 28

Struggling against the hands that held him flat to the ground, Branigan fought to rise, to escape, his head tossing as he did so. He didn't understand what had happened or where he was. He didn't hear the click of the shackles around his ankles, but felt the cold of the metal against his skin through his socks.

The men holding him finally stood, winded from their fight with him. They had not expected him to awake so soon or to fight them so hard to escape. The older man, heavyset, his face lined with the abuses he had put his body through, the scraggly beard hiding the lower face, shook his head and pointed to the table, his words muttered from a mouth that held broken and stained teeth.

The younger man, on his way to the same state of body, reached for the syringe, their orders specific. First, the shackles, then the sedative. Their employer wanted him docile. Why, they really didn't care. All they cared about was the money they were being paid.

Branigan fought the men again as his arm was held to the ground, the syringe plunging in, a press on the end sending the sedative into his unwilling body. His body twisted as his other hand reached for the syringe to try and grasp it, reached to shove the men away from him, his head raising in his determination to succeed. But his determination and fight were not enough. The sedative began its work, and his body collapsed, his head hitting hard on the concrete floor he was laying on, his eyes rolling back as his consciousness fled. His body relaxed, all fight gone. He could only murmur, God, please help me before he dropped down into a well of darkness.

The men stood, shaking their heads at him. Neither had expected the fight from him, not after the blow he took that rendered him unconscious. They walked away, the door slamming shut behind them. There was no need for a lock. His shackles' chain traced its way across the cold, dirty concrete floor to end in a huge eye hook in the wall. He would not escape, that they were confident of.

Their employer turned from the window she was staring out of, anger on her face and in her eyes, disdain for the men in front of her hidden. If she could work in any other way, she would, but she needed them, and she had to acknowledge that they needed her.

"Well?" Her voice was low and harsh, not fitting the groomed appearance she endeavoured to portray.

"He's out. He fought us. He shouldn't have been awake. The shackles are in place, and the sedative given." The older man spoke, not looking up as he did so. He had learned that he didn't look at her. The blows from her hands and cane had taught him that.

"Good. Now comes the next part." She walked towards him, her cane tapping on the floor as it helped her to balance. "We will need to take pictures of him and send them to that witch."

The younger man shrugged, reaching for the camera, and following as she walked towards where Branigan was held captive. She stood, staring down at him, her cane tapping at his chest, finding he didn't move.

"Good. Good." She looked around. "There. By that pile of broken blocks. Lean him against that."

The two men exchanged glances before shrugging once more. The younger man set the camera down and helped to drag Branigan to the pile of debris, positioning as she directed, more than once, until she was satisfied. His body sagged against the blocks, his head hanging to the side, his hair disheveled, the bruising on his face evident in the bright light the older man had been handed and ordered to shine on him.

The younger man approached, camera in hand, hesitating for the barest second before the camera clicked through a number of shots. She reached for the camera, almost tearing it away from him in her eagerness to see the pictures, scrolling through them, finding the ones that she wanted, and deleting the others. Camera in her hand, she turned, walking away, the cane tapping once more on the concrete before the men heard it tapping up the rough stairs to the main floor and then across the floor to the office she had set up.

The younger man shook his head. Somehow, this was not what he had signed on for. Not at all. He shot a look at his partner who was standing, staring down at Branigan, before he turned, quietly moving away, finding the door to the outside and once through it, closing it quietly behind him. He was done, he thought. He would pack up the room he rented and leave this town, this very night. He would be gone before anyone found out about it. A new start in a new province. That was what he had decided to do.

The woman finally turned from her desk, reaching for the photos on the printer, satisfied with the ones she had selected. She hunted for a large Manila envelope, addressing it to Guenivere in large black block letters, intending to drop it into the mail that night. It would find her. She would be watching for her reaction, hearing of it from her source. She cackled with glee. It was all starting to come together, her plots and plans for revenge. The Danby's would be destroyed through all this, and that was her end goal. Take them down. Wreak havoc on their lives. Destroy their livelihood. She had many plots and plans to put in place, but they depended on the reaction she would elicit from these photos.

Chapter 29

Two days later, Brett fingered the envelope that had appeared on the reception desk in the office, not sure who or when it had appeared. He didn't remember seeing it the day before, but then, he had not looked at the mail. He sighed, knowing he had to find Guenivere and just not sure where she would be. He detoured by the mechanic shop for a quick word with Douglas and then headed for his car, determined to find his daughter.

Guenivere looked up from the papers she was studying, deep into research on the Langs, as she heard the door to the conference room open. Some of the men were there, each deep into their own research, quiet words and sometimes jokes flying between them. She frowned as her father appeared.

"Dad?" She went to stand but Brett shook his head, taking a seat beside her. "What do you have?"

"I have no idea, Guenivere. I found it on the desk out front this morning. I don't know when it was delivered but it could have been yesterday or even this morning. I was back and forth from the shop and I must admit, I didn't always lock the door, and I should have."

Guenivere shrugged. "They would have just shoved it into the box." She reached reluctant hands for it. "It doesn't look too important. I'll get to it in a bit. I have some information here I'm trying to understand and I think I have found a link of some kind. I want to talk to you about it when I'm done."

Brett studied her for a moment, knowing from experience that she would not open the envelope until she was ready to. He rose, heading for the coffee pot, and then taking a seat near Brody, who was staring at a computer screen.

"It won't bite, Brody."

Brody's head shot around as Brett spoke, finally realizing he wasn't alone, and then grinning at the words. "It won't? Here, along I've been wrong. I was convinced it would. What brings you out?"

"I had an envelope to bring to Guenivere." He leaned back to look over at his daughter. "She hasn't opened it yet. She won't until she's ready, and who knows when that will be."

"Was it important?"

Brett shrugged. "I doubt it. Probably just some advertising for her. She gets that all the time and just throws it away. It has come to the point, she'll look at an envelope and most times won't even touch it."

"That's not good, especially now. That's how they may communicate with her."

"She knows that, Brody. Part of it is denial on her side. We've tried to talk to her, Lena and I. It doesn't make any difference. Tell me, where are you all in the mystery? Any word on Branigan?"

"No, there hasn't been. I don't like that. There should be." Brody was off on a tangent, turning back to his computer, completely forgetting that Brett was waiting for an answer.

Brett pulled out his phone, scrolling through his business emails, and was soon concentrating on them, the noise and conversation in the room fading to the background. He had looked up on occasion towards Guenivere but found her head bent over the papers in front of her.

A sudden scream split the air in the room about an hour after Brett had entered, the sound of a chair violently shoved across the floor clattering as did the sound of a body hitting the floor as the chair crashed to its side, startling the men, having them on their feet in instant, eyes alert to what had happened. Brody spun and then was across the room, on his knees beside Guenivere, who lay on her side, reaching to try and raise her to a sitting position. She lay, curled up, her arms tight around her head, sobs wracking her body.

Brett was there, on his knees on her other side, hands reaching for her as well, drawing back as she flew to her hands and knees and scrambled away from them, to tuck herself into a corner, her knees drawn up, her face buried against them, her arms once more wrapped around her head.

"What happened?" Brett's voice was harsh, as he stared at his daughter, afraid to approach her, afraid not to.

Brady stood by the table, his eyes on the envelope. "Where did this come from?"

Brett rose, fear in his heart for the young couple. "It was at the office. I brought it over to her. Why?"

Brady's pen was out to move the photos of Branigan that had dumped out of the envelope, as Blair and Breck stood behind him, their faces as grim as they could get. "This is why. It's Branigan."

"What?" Brett was at the table, his eyes on the photos, before they slid shut. "I didn't know. I thought it was just advertising, like she's had before." He spun and then was across the room, on his knees beside his daughter, a hand hovering in mid-air as he reached to touch her and then paused.

Brady was beside him, his own hands reaching for Guenivere, moving her arms and then scooping her up into his arms, leaving the room almost on a run, Brett behind him, Braydon running to find Doc and Anna, who were around that day.

Doc stood for a moment in the infirmary doorway, before he approached Guenivere.

"What happened?" When Brett had explained, Doc shook his head. "I see. Let Anna and I have some time with her, Brett, and then I'll have you come back in. You'll need to find Lena."

Brady spoke up. "Blair was on his way to get her."

"Good. Now, clear the room." Doc watched as the door closed behind them before he turned to Anna. "I don't like this, Anna. She's at her limit. This may push her over it."

"I know, Doc. That I do know." Anna's hand stroked down Guenivere's hair. "I've been praying so hard for her. I could see the hope rising in her, hope I haven't seen in her before. Now this. It will set her back."

"I am afraid it will. We need to pray for her and pray hard."

Guenivere roused, her eyes staring around in fright until she focused on Anna. "Anna? Where's Branigan?"

"He's not here, Guenivere. Don't you remember?"

Guenivere's eyes slid shut, as tears flowed. "I do. I am so afraid. I think he was dead in those pictures. Please? Dear Lord, please. Don't let him be dead."

Anna and Doc shared a startled look before Doc was out the door, finding Brett and Breck right outside.

"Those pictures? What was in them?"

Brett shuddered. "Branigan. He was slumped over some broken concrete blocks, I think. He looked dead, but I'm sure that can't be." Brett's face paled even more. "He was shackled, Doc. There was a close up on his ankles. Who does that?" A hand clutched at his chest.

Breck had watched Brett closely, his arms reaching to catch him as he collapsed to the floor, Doc beside him.

"Into the other room, Breck. And then call for the paramedics. I think it's his heart."

Breck lifted Brett and carried him to the other room, then stood, phone in hand as he made the call, watching as Doc worked on their friend. He turned at a tap before the door open, and Brody appeared.

"Breck?"

"We think it's his heart. We have people on the way."

Brock grew stern. "This is not what they need. I'll have Blair change course and head to the hospital with Lena." He stood back as the paramedics entered, watching as they worked on Brett before shifting him to their stretcher and then walking rapidly away, the heart monitor on the stretcher between Brett's feet, the oxygen mask in place. The men and ladies from the building stood, horror and concern on their faces before Breck was away, following the ambulance as siren wailing and emergency lights flashing it sped for the hospital.

Barnabas stood near Doc, his hand on the older man's shoulder, a prayer rising for Brett, Lena and Guenivere.

"Doc?"

"I think it was his heart. They'll assess him. Guenivere? Now, this is not going to help her. She's on the edge, Barnabas. She can't take much more. Those photos almost destroyed her."

"That's what Brady said. He's heading to find Dallas with them. Whoever this is, they're brutal."

Doc hesitated before he spoke. "Somehow, I think you'll find it's a woman. They can have a real cruel streak. This had all the earmarks of that."

Barnabas stared at him before he nodded. "I think you're right, Doc. I really do. And it's someone we know."

"That's what I'm afraid of. I'm going to pull out that church directory. I heard Guenivere's comments and I have a feeling she's right." Doc walked away, his steps as heavy as his heart.

Chapter 30

Late that same afternoon, Guenivere stood beside her father's hospital bed, her arm around her mother, her eyes studying the monitors connected to him even as the beeps sounded in her ears. They had been lucky, the Emergency Room doctor had declared, even as Lena shook her head and stated emphatically that it was God, not luck. Guenivere had roused in the infirmary in the Foundation building, overhearing Doc's quiet conversation with Anna. She had been on her feet, flying from the room, desperate to find her way to the hospital. Bradon and Brendon were there, rushing her to Bradon's truck, shoving her inside and then speeding as quickly as they could for the hospital.

Guenivere had sat, silent, still, her hands clasped together, even as the men had each taken turns to watch her. She had flown into the Emergency department, finding her mother waiting, Blair hovering near, and was enveloped in her mother's arms. They had finally been taken to Brett's room, the additional comment being that he would be kept in overnight and that he needed to reduce the stress in his life. Guenivere had given a harsh laugh at that, surprising the doctor, and then swallowed hard, suppressing her feelings.

Barnabas watched for a moment from the doorway before he approached, his hand resting lightly on Lena's shoulder.

"Lena?"

"He can go home tomorrow, Barnabas. God was good. It wasn't a heart attack, just stress. The doctor wants to do more testing, but it can be done as an outpatient."

"That's good." He looked past her mother at Guenivere, finding her watching him. "If you like, we can set you up at the building."

Lena shook her head. "No, he'll want to go home. But we can't have Guenivere there. They'll use this to get at her."

"I'm sure they will." Barnabas shook his head in warning as Guenivere opened her mouth, biting back a smile as she snapped it closed, a frown on her face.

"Mom? I can't stay away."

"You must, Guenivere. You must." She looked up at Barnabas. "Barnabas? Please?"

"She's right, Guenivere. They will use this to get to you. This may be all part of the plan, you know."

Guenivere blew out a breath, before she nodded. "I know. I just don't want to be away from Dad." She looked down as she felt a hand cover the one she had resting on the bed beside her father. "Dad? You're awake?"

"I am, Guenivere. I've been laying here, listening and thinking. Barnabas is right. This may be part of their overall plan. If we can keep apart, maybe they will back away. Please stay at the building. You have security there." His finger raised as she went to protest. "I know. Security has been breached.

Branigan was taken from there. But it is still likely the safest place for you. Barnabas, the photos?"

"Dallas has them. He's quite disturbed at them, but quite determined to find Branigan. He got word to me that officers are volunteering their off-duty hours to help. Branigan has been there for so many of them over the years with his work as an auxiliary officer."

"He has been. That's good. I pray it's resolved soon." His eyes closing, Brett drifted off to sleep.

Lena turned to Guenivere. "Go on with Barnabas, dear. I'm not leaving but I would feel better knowing you're safe."

Guenivere was torn. She wanted to stay with her parents but she always wanted to be out hunting for Branigan. Neither option seemed available to her, and she felt angry and disgruntled. She hugged her mother, following Barnabas as he led the way out to his car, tucking her inside, before he stood, staring around, not liking that he felt watched. He nodded at the security team that waited in the two vehicles, and pulled away from the hospital, one car in front, the other behind. He was taking no chances, not any more. Whoever it was had proven that they would and could play dirty. Lord, we need to end this. This could have ended today in tragedy. I don't want that for this family. Please, Lord?

Guenivere glared at the clock in her living room for the umpteenth time. She sighed. It was early morning, and she had not slept, instead spending her time pacing, moving from room to room. She had sought her bed, only to toss and turn, rising to pace, and then to seek her bed once more. This was not working, she thought, slouching down on the couch, her arms crossed over her chest, her chin dropping down with her hair covering her face. She stayed like that as she thought through what she knew, her hands finally coming up to grasp her hair and pull at it.

There has to be an answer somewhere, she thought. Lord, right about now would be a good time to send a hint or two. Her head dropped back and rested on the couch back, and her eyes closed. She envisioned the photos, cringing in fear once more for Branigan, praying that he really was alive and would come back to her. She was losing hope, she knew, and that she didn't like or even want.

Her mind drifted back to when she was twelve and that incident. She frowned as she tried to remember who had been there. Her brow cleared as she shuddered. She had a good idea now who was behind everything. She just had to prove it, and how to do that, she had no idea. She needed to talk to someone and was on her feet, almost running for the door, when she slid to a stop. No, she couldn't awaken anyone in the middle of the night.

She spun, heading for the kitchen, reaching for the carafe to rinse it out and then dumping the water into the coffee pot, knowing she would need it. She reached for the bread on the counter and then the tomato and lettuce from the fridge, fixing her favourite sandwich. She slapped it down harder than she meant to onto a place, reaching for a mug, then reaching past that one for the largest one she could find in the cupboard. Her hand stilled as she caught the verse on it. Psalms, she thought: *I hope in Your word.* She smiled. Branigan must have put it there. I have to ask him that.

Guenivere walked rapidly through to her office, setting down the plate and her mug, pulling up her chair. She sighed. The anger, guilt and despair that she felt was weighing her down. She needed to spend time with God before she did anything else. Her head went down on her arms as she wept, prayed, and then waited.

Chapter 31

Early morning found Guenivere running down the stairs, heading for the conference room, a thought having crossed her mind. She clutched a sheaf of papers in her hand, her other hand sliding lightly down the railing. Breck watched from where he stood near the front doors, dressed for his morning run. He hesitated before shaking his head. He would check in on her when he returned.

Guenivere slipped quietly into the room, her hand reaching to flip on the light switches, hesitating for a moment as the fear from the day before overcame her once more. She shook her head, stiffened her spine, and marched towards the computer she had been using. Booting it up, she hesitated, her hands hovering over the keyboard, her eyes looking up. *Lord, I know what I think, who I think it is. I just don't know for sure. I need proof, and it's too well hidden. I need You to step in for me. Please, Lord? I don't know if Branigan is still alive or if he's dead. The pictures tell me that he is dead, my heart says otherwise. Guide our search. We need to find them, whoever it is, and then find him.*

Brennen paused as he passed the door a couple of hours later, hearing muttering and then humming coming out through the partially open door. He frowned, and then reached to shove the door open further, looking down at the sneaker holding it open. He grinned, bending to pick up the peach-coloured shoe. Guenivere, he thought. She's in here working, and propped the door open to watch for one of us.

He didn't try to hide his footsteps as he walked across the room, but actually walked a little harder than usual, an amused look crossing his face as Guenivere ignored him. He came to a stop next to her, his mouth open to speak, when her forefinger went up into the air in an abrupt manner, stopping his words, but causing the amusement on his face to deepen. He dropped into a chair beside her, his elbow on the table, head on his hand as he tilted it to watch her face. He frowned at the deep concentration, and then smiled inwardly at the streak of dust on her cheek. What have you been doing, Guenivere, that you found dust? I thought the room was clean.

"Brennen? What is your take on this?" Guenivere suddenly spoke, shoving papers across to him hard enough that he had to slap a hand down on them to stop them from flying from the table.

"What is this?"

"A mess, I think. I need someone to take a look at it, someone who really doesn't know the people involved. That would be one of you." Guenivere turned to face him, devastation showing deep in her eyes. "I know what I think it says, and I know what I don't it to say."

"That doesn't make sense, Guenivere." Brennen frowned at her, his eyes lifting to look past her as he heard a sound at the door, and Brandon, Brendon and Brody appeared, shortly followed by Blair, Bradon and Baird.

"What did you find?"

She shook her head. "Read it, please. Then, talk to me." She dropped her head to her folded arms and the sigh she drew shook her body, causing the men to stare at her before staring at one another.

"Brennen?" Blair finally spoke, even as he slid into a chair, and reached for the keyboard and mouse of the computer he had selected.

"Guenivere has been hard at work, I would say for hours." He gathered up the sheaf of papers and held it up, drawing the men's eyes to first it and then Guenivere. "She's come up with something she needs verified. We can do that, can't we?"

"We can." Baird reached for the papers. "Let me make copies for each of us. Then, each of us can work on it, and pool our thoughts. That's how we do it, Guenivere."

She nodded without raising her head. "I know. It's just I don't like what I found." Her voice was muffled, low enough that they had to strain to catch her words.

The men were soon deep in concentration, amazed at what Guenivere had been able to dig up, but dismay rippling through the room as the people she had named. It would be difficult, Brennen thought, to find the evidence, and he thought he knew Guenivere well enough that she wouldn't say anything without it.

"Guenivere?" When she looked up, Blair smiled. "You've done a lot and just in a short while."

"No, actually. I have been working on it since around two, I think. I did what I could on my own system, but you have programs here that I needed to use." She paled, a thought crossing her mind. "I'm sorry. I shouldn't have used them." She shoved at the table, preparatory to rising and running from the room.

Breck's hand on her back stopped her even though it caused her to jump.

"There is no problem, not that I can see, Guenivere. Those programs are open for any of us to use, us men, the ladies of the family. And believe me, you are one of us, whether you realize it or not. Branigan has staked his claim on you." He paused, as he watched tears pool in her eyes. "Guenivere? What did I say?"

She simply shook her head, overcome by her emotions for a moment, not seeing Cadee until Cadee's arm encircled her shoulders. She looked up, seeing the five younger women had entered as had the rest of the men.

Guenivere sighed to herself. She had to be honest with them, didn't she, Lord? And how did she do just that? Branigan should be the one stating the obvious. They were his friends, those he considered his family.

Looking around at them all, her eyes resting on Barnabas, seeing the knowledge of what she was about to say in his eyes, she sighed once more and then reached for the chain around her neck, pulling it out from under the soft yellow T-shirt she wore.

She didn't look around, afraid of the censure she would see. Cadee reached for the ring on the chain, studying it and then reaching to unclasp the chain, to slide the ruby and gold ring from it. She held it out to her friend.

"Put it on, Guenivere. Put it on where Branigan placed it. He would want to acknowledge that you are his chosen life mate, his helpmeet, his love."

Guenivere had turned to watch her, seeing the acceptance in her friend's face, before she reached to take the ring, her eyes searching each one in the room, finding love and acceptance, not the censure she expected, on each face.

Barnabas nodded as she once more sought him out. "Do what Cadee asked, Guenivere. Branigan would want you to. Don't hide from us. We are, each one of us, trying our best to solve this and bring him home to you. And we will bring him home. That's a guarantee. God has spoken and He is not done with Branigan. Not yet."

Chapter 32

A groan pulled deep from within him, Branigan roused in the early morning hours, feeling around for his blankets to pull up over him against the early morning chill. For some reason, he thought, I can't find them. That's bizarre. He roused a bit more and wondered at the lumpy hard mattress he was laying on, that had sharp corners driving into him as he shifted. He finally pushed himself to a sitting position, leaning back on what he thought was the headboard, but it too felt odd. It has too hard for the wooden headboard he had, and too cold. His head spun from his efforts and his eyes slid closed to counter the vertigo assailing him.

Branigan rubbed at his face, feeling the stubble from two days of not shaving. This can't be right, he thought. Guenivere and I had dinner out last night, before walking by the river. His mind drifted back to their dinner.

He had chosen a small family-run British restaurant, a favourite of his, and as it turned out, one of Gueinvere's as well. They had lingered over their meal, their conversation quiet at times and at times somewhat heated as they got to know one another better.

Branigan had reached for her hand as they left, steering her towards a park near there, mingling with the pedestrians until he found the bench he favoured.

She had nestled down in his arms, content, she said, just to be there and with him.

Talk had been intermittent before he bit at his lip, staring off towards the town. His gaze dropped to her, her profile to him as she laughed at the antics of some small children and their dog nearby.

"Guenivere?" His voice was low and hesitant enough that she turned to him, a question on her lips that died away as she searched his face. "I know we haven't know each other long. I mean, we've been dating. We have talked, I think, about so many things. I love your spirit, your thoughts, your willingness to tell me off, to forgive, your eagerness for life. I see the change in you. God is restoring your hope." He paused, drawing his upper lip in, before he continued. "I guess what I am trying to say is this. I love you, deeply, and more each day. Will you be mine, to share life with me, to walk beside me, to serve God wherever He would direct us? Will you be my Proverbs 31 lady?" He held up the single ruby ring that had been his mother's, given to him by his father when he was in his teens, to be given, his father said with a sad but loving smile, to the lady who would be his Proverbs 31 lady, just as Branigan's mother had been his.

Guenivere swallowed hard, not believing that he had asked, before she looked away, trying to control her unruly emotions. She felt, rather than saw, the motion of his hand dropping, and could sense the disappointment he felt.

Turning back, she simply nodded, her hand going out to grasp his.

"I will, Branigan. I will. I like what you said. Dad has always described Mom as that."

"He has? That's how Dad looked at my mother. I don't have the memories of her that you do of your mother." He slipped on her ring and then gathered her close.

Branigan had frowned as she slipped it onto a chain, a question on his face.

"It's okay. I will wear it, but we need to talk to Mom and Dad first, unless you have already."

He shook his head at that and then agreed with her, with the stipulation that she would be wearing it on her finger for everyone to see by the next evening.

Branigan's mind drifted back to the present, a groan rising from him again as he tried to raise himself up and stand. He was finally able to draw himself to his feet, a hand planted on the wall, his blurry eyes staring around.

He frowned as he stared down at the pile of broken blocks and wondered just how he had gotten to there. It certainly wasn't his apartment, that much he knew, but where he was? That was the question it seemed he could not answer. God? Are You there? Do You know where I am? Of course, You do. You're God. You would know that. His thoughts were not the usual organized thoughts he had but scattered and incomplete.

He turned to walk away, surprise on his face that he could not take a normal step. He frowned at the clank of metal as he once more stepped forward, heading towards the door he could see just a few feet away.

Branigan stared at his face, seeing the bruise on his jaw. How did I do that, he thought? I look like I have been in a fight or something. Running the tap to warm the water, he splashed his face, reaching for a towel to dry it off.

He turned, once more restricted in his steps, the clanging of metal sounding loud in his eyes, echoing through the small room, and intensifying the headache that was pounding in his temples and behind his eyes.

Slumping back to the floor, Branigan stared at his ankles, not quite sure of what he was seeing before he reached to touch and then grasp the shackles binding him. He shook them and then felt for a way to remove them, finding none. What did I do, he wondered? Just where am I?

His head raised as he searched the room, seeing the tray near him with food and a bottle of water. He reached for the water, twisted off the cap, and drank deeply, before he reached for the sandwich, downing it in a few bites. He had no idea what day it was, and no way of finding out. Finished his meal, his hand still holding the partly-full water bottle, his head went back against the wall and he slept, not hearing the door open and the older man enter.

The man stood, his eyes narrowed as he studied first Branigan and then the tray. He nodded. Good, he thought. He did eat and drink. We need him to do that, to wake up and stay alive. He reached for the tray to retrieve it and then for the water bottle before shaking his head. That wouldn't hurt to stay. He could not defend himself with that.

The door swung shut and the lock snapped into place, Branigan rousing slightly at the noise before he drifted off once more. His thoughts became muddled dreams where he was being chased or he was chasing an unknown opponent. He could hear Guenivere's voice calling to him and in his drugged sleep he reached for her, calling her name, before he lurched forward to stand and then fall with a heavy hard thud to the concrete floor, his arms askew over his head. He lay there, for unknown hours, before the man returned with a new tray, this time near dusk.

Chapter 33

His back to the door, Branigan listened to the commands being thrown at him by the older man. He simply shook his head. There was no way, he thought, that he would do anything that would endanger Guenivere, her family, their business or his friends. That was a given.

The man was growing angry. Pressure was being put on him to make Branigan agree. Secretly, he admired the younger man, but he was making it extremely difficult for him to do what he had been charged to do.

"You will make that video. And you will provide the information we need for the security system that you changed. We will have access to their trucks." The man stormed from the room, the door slamming closed behind him.

Branigan drew in a deep breath and let it out slowly. It was what he had thought. They wanted access to Brett's fleet and that would be for likely smuggling or illegal activities of some kind. How did he get away from them and warn Brett?

Lord, I don't know how to do this. Only You can release me and help me to stop this.

He turned to eye the door, knowing he could not reach it, before he began to pace in the little room that he could. He finally slumped back down to the floor, his eyes closing as he slept. He didn't realize that he had been drugged again, part of the way that they were trying to wear him down, to make him pliable in their hands and an accessory to their devious, dirty plans. He didn't know who all they were planning on ensnaring.

The woman stood in the doorway, anger radiating from her. They were on a time crunch, her words lashing at the man standing behind her.

"I don't care how you accomplish it. He will make that video. He will provide the information that we need." She stormed away, her cane tapping in tune with her angry, heavy footsteps, leaving the man staring after her before he moved to the doorway.

"There ain't no way he'll do it." The whine sounded deep in his voice. "There just ain't no way."

Days went by like this, Branigan growing more exhausted and fatigued, the shackles wearing heavy on his ankles, the sore spots appearing where they rubbed. He resolutely refused to do what they asked, simply stating that he couldn't and wouldn't be part of their schemes to destroy a family, a respected business, or his friends. He just turned away from their requests, to stand leaning against the wall, his eyes fastened on the small dirty window that let in what light it could to brighten his day and to make the nights seem shorter.

Finally, the day came. It had been how long, Branigan couldn't tell. He had lost track of time, of days, just knowing that night followed day which followed night. He had paced where he could, tried to free himself from his shackles, had sleep, both a natural sleep and a drugged one. He had been threatened, cajoled, promised freedom if he would only help. Guenivere and her family and then his friends and their ladies had been threatened. He had simply shaken his head and backed away, to stand staring up at the window. Branigan had managed to reach it one day by standing on his toes and using a wet rag had cleaned what he could. It had make his dungeon brighter to a degree. And that was what he was in, a dungeon.

His mind had slipped one day, back to when he was a small boy, and playing cops and robbers with his friends had been their best past-time. His father had smiled at him and then sat him down, explaining what it was like to be one of the good guys and what it was like to be one of the bad guys, as he put it. His explanation had made Branigan determined to be one of the good guys. That was what he had promised his father that day, causing his father to smile and then hug him. Branigan had sat that day, in his prison, his eyes riveted on the door as he thought about that and then remembered how his father had talked about Paul being in a dungeon, that he had still served God there, had praised and prayed, had sent out encouragement to the churches. He had not lost hope. Branigan was determined that he would be the same. He would not lose hope, as difficult as it seemed.

Branigan had grown thin, his face covered in a rough beard, his thoughts on his beloved and how she would be coping. She would have the support of all his friends, he knew, as well as the Foundation board, to say nothing of her parents.

He thought about the board, a frown on his face as he searched his memory, before a groan shook his body and his eyes closed. That was the voice he had kept hearing, in his dreams, outside his dungeon. It was that board member. But how did he let them know? How did he reach out to his friends?

Entering the room in the near dusk of that day, the man searched for Branigan, not seeing him at first. Curses flew from his mouth as he headed back out to find a flashlight, shining it around as he searched. Branigan was gone, the shackles he had been wearing cut open and laying discarded on the floor. The man paled, curses flying anew from him, as he searched the room and then backed out, to slam the door and look at the lock. He couldn't tell if it had been tampered with, he had scratched it so badly with his alcohol-shaky hands. He turned, heading for the stairs, and then the back door, searching for Branigan, and not finding him.

He stood, as the moonlight became to filter through the trees, his mind blurring, but the cunning he had been known for all his life still active. He spun to stare at the house, and then spun, running for his truck, the gravel in the driveway spewing from the tires as he gunned the motor and fled. He had had enough, he decided, and would leave town, just like the younger man had. He wouldn't even wait to collect what he had in his apartment. There was nothing there of value and nothing that would identify him. He had used fake identification to rent it.

Cane tapping on the stairs, the woman approached the door herself. She had appeared, calling for her henchman and not receiving an answer from him. Anger had begun to build at him and then at Branigan and then at Brett and his trucking company. She stood for a moment, shocked to see the door unlocked and open, before she shoved at it with her cane and waited, finally entering, to find it empty, to find the man she had planned to use, destroy and then kill missing. Rage began to build as she turned for the stairs, her balance unsteady under it. She tottered on the next to the top step, her balance gone, and she plunged back down the steps, to lie, a crumpled, broken heap that no one would miss or no one might ever find.

Chapter 34

Guenivere rose from her seat that day they had discovered her engagement, stretching. She glanced at the clock in shock. She had been settled there for hours, it would appear, and she realized that she was both hungry and thirsty. A hand on her arm turned her towards Ennis, who pulled her with her out of the conference room and to her own apartment. Guenivere stood for a moment, staring at the ladies seated in the living room, her own mother one of them, as well as Anna and her sister, Amy.

"What is going on, Ennis?" She turned to her friend, a puzzled look on her face.

Ennis had just grinned. "We needed to rescue you, that's what. First, you haven't moved from there for hours. I hear you were already working before the guys entered. And that you were up at two working away. You need to eat. Branigan would expect that of you."

Soberly, Guenivere turned to each lady, catching their nods of agreement but something more. She sank down beside her mother, sitting on the floor, her legs folded, as her mother's hand rested on her head.

"Who's with Dad?"

"Doc. He appeared, sent me off with Baird, who told me I was to come here for lunch." She studied her daughter, seeing the strain and stress in her face, but something more. A hope in something or someone, she thought. "He seems to think I needed to talk with you."

Guenivere sighed. "I wanted to tell you the other night when you called, but Branigan and I planned to surprise you with a meal last night. That didn't happen." She held up her hand for her mother to take, hearing the soft intake of her breath. "He calls me his Proverbs 31 lady, just like Dad does with you. He said his father did the same."

Lena reached to hug her daughter, a few tears falling on Guenivere's hair, before she pulled back. "Dad suspected something like this. He said Branigan had approached him one day but wouldn't say why. This must have been it." She looked up at a sound from Fynn.

Guenivere looked around her mother at Fynn. "Fynn? You're up to something. All of you."

The ladies laughed before Berneen spoke. "We are. We know you're missing Branigan and that you're determined to find him. We've been talking. As you know, I married Baird to save his life. Cadee married Benen to escape from a war-torn country. Devaney and Blair were engaged but she walked away to save his life. Ennis and Fynn had a chance to be courted, as they used to say. You're different. You're being courted, but there is also something else going on that we can't understand right now." She paused, biting at her lip, distress on her face. "Maybe this wasn't such a good idea, after all."

Guenivere was puzzled. "What wasn't such a good idea?"

Devaney spoke up. "We just thought, to help you get through this, that we could sort of, you know, help you plan."

"So definite there, Devaney." Cadee grinned at her friend. "What Devaney is stumbling over her words, trying to say, is that we would like to help you put some ideas down for your wedding. I know Branigan and he would say to go for it. He wouldn't care, as long as you were there. In fact, if you showed up in your jeans, a T-shirt and your peach sneakers, he'd still marry you."

The ladies laughed as Guenivere sat back, her eyes wide, her mouth open until she snapped it closed. She felt her mother's arm around her.

"I think it's a wonderful idea, Guenivere. We've talked over the years about what you'd like. I know your heart. You want simple and plain. Let's see what we can come up with. You don't have to do anything we say, but if you would listen and then plan from that, it will help. It will keep your hope up that he's coming back. And he is. I am confident of that."

Much laughter filled the room as the most outrageous ideas were thrown at her. Guenivere suspected they were doing that on purpose, trying to outdo one another.

She finally rose, tucking the notes she had made into the folder handed to her, and walked down the stairs and out to where Benen was waiting for her. She stood, arms folded around herself, as her mother left, tears near the surface, not seeing both Barnabas and Buckley watching her.

Barnabas approached and with the ease of an old friendship, dropped an arm around her shoulder. Buckley stood on her other side.

"Well? We passed by the apartment. You ladies sounded like you were having fun." Barnabas grinned down at her.

She shook her head. "Did you put them up to having me there for lunch and bringing in Mom and Anna and Amy?"

Both men shook their heads.

"No, that was their idea. Fynn did ask if we thought they should, and we agreed. You needed a break, Guenivere, and we weren't sure you would take one." Buckley peered down at the folder in her hand. "It looks as if it was a productive lunch."

"In some ways, it was. They are all so sweet. They wanted to help me come up with ideas for the wedding. Only, I don't know that there will be one." She ran from them, unable to stem the flow of tears, the lobby door shutting silently behind her as she ran for her apartment.

Barnabas and Buckley stared after her before they looked at one another.

"It had to happen, Barnabas. She's been on edge now for days."

Barnabas agree. "It did. We've all tried to get her to take a break, to slow down, but she won't. She wants this over and Branigan home." He ran his hand through his hair. "Dad's heading out this way tonight. We need to talk with him about what we've found. As the Board chair, he needs to know and help to make plans on where we go with this."

"That he does. Let's plan on meeting in your office, spending some time in prayer, and then working through what we have. We don't want to go to the Board yet, not until we have absolute proof."

"No, we can't. Guenivere is right in that respect. No accusations without proof. We'll likely need to call in Will in his official capacity at some point."

"That we will." Buckley opened his mouth to speak again, then shut it, shaking his head before he walked away.

Chapter 35

Days passed, and Guenivere grew thin and pale. She slept but she knew her sleep was restless. She would wake early in the morning and just lie in bed, her thoughts on Branigan, her heart in prayer, before she would rise, dress, grab a piece of toast or bagel, and then head for the conference room. Her parents had each taken her aside, and tried to talk to her, but she had just stared past them and continued as she was. Her work for her father was still done, but she didn't have the heart or interest in it any more.

That particular day, she had roused early, glancing at the clock to see that it was only three. She had closed her eyes, seeking her rest again, but unable to find it. Finally rising, she had taken her Bible and a mug of tea this time, and headed for her balcony, to spend the next few hours seeking every verse she could find on hope and praying them through.

Buckley had looked up as she entered the conference room, ready to joke with her as he usually did, but he didn't. There was something different about her that day, he thought. I wonder what.

He finally rose and took a seat beside her, his head tilted to study her face. Guenivere knew he was there and looked over at him.

"Buckley?"

"Guenivere. Something has changed."

She sighed as she sat back in her chair, a pen tapping on the table. "I don't know, Buckley. I had a horrible feeling about three this morning and just had to get up. I looked up all the verses on hope that I could find." She looked over at him, seeing him nodding. "Does that make any sense at all?"

"It does. Sometimes God will wake us when we need to spend time with Him. I have often woken for days at a certain time, unsure why, but praying through the friends I have, the church family, and just situations that I am aware of. He doesn't expect us to have the answers. He just wants us to search and be willing to listen."

"He does." She looked past him. "I just wish I knew where Branigan was and if he's okay. It's seems so long since he was taken."

"It has been. Not so much in days, but in worry, in stress, in the unknown. In lost hope." He nodded as her gaze came back to him. "That's been a difficulty for you to accept. That you can and have lost hope but God will restore that."

"He has, Barnabas." Guenivere looked past him once more as the door opened and Barnabas appeared with a man she didn't know. "Buckley, who's that?"

He spun on his chair, and then was on his feet, his hand outstretched. "Murphy O'Brien? What brings you here?"

Murphy grinned. He was a friend of Fynn's, a team member for Abe Finlay, who ran a security team. Abe's wife, Emma, had been involved in the search for

Branigan, coming aboard to the investigation at Fynn's request.

"To see you all?" He grinned again as Buckley laughed, before he sobered. He walked over to stand in front of Guenivere, who had risen to her feet, her hands clutched in front of her. "This lady brings me here."

"I'm sorry, I don't think I know you."

"You don't. You know my name. What you don't know is that I am employed by a security team. You have heard Fynn speak of Abe and Emma?" At her nod, he continued. "Abe is my employer, or more accurately, I am his partner. He got word yesterday about something and we headed this way today." His hand gently took her arm and seated her, seating himself in the chair Buckley had abandoned. "Abe asked me to come and find you. He wanted one of us to talk to you in person."

Guenivere was staring at him, seeking an answer, seeing something in his eyes and face that gave her hope. "Branigan? Is it Branigan? Do you know where he is? Have you found him? Can you take me to him?"

Murphy gave a quick grin that didn't reach his eyes. "That's why I'm here. I do know where Branigan is. And yes, I can and will take you there." His hand reached out to steady her as she wobbled on her chair. "He's safe, Guenivere. We have him and he's safe."

"Oh, thank You, Lord." Her eyes slid closed as she endeavored to control her emotions before they popped open. "What time?"

"I'm sorry. What do you mean?" Murphy didn't understand how she asked that, instead of how Branigan was.

"What time? What time did you find him and get him out?"

"What time? Somewhere around three this morning." He looked genuinely puzzled as she began to sob, her head down on her folded arms on the table. He looked up at Buckley, who stood, a hand resting on her shoulder. "What did I say?"

"She awoke this morning at that time, and felt compelled to search the scriptures for verses on hope. She somehow knew."

Murphy shook his head. "God does indeed work in mysterious ways. I always say He has a plan and purpose for us we don't know about. Who knows why they had to go through this?'

"He's alive? Please, tell me he's alive." The desperate pleading in her voice broke the men's hearts.

"He is, Guenivere. He roused a bit and tried to fight us, but he didn't stay awake for long." His heart broke for her as she wept, turning as she felt her father beside her, to be hugged to him as she had been when she was a child and hurt.

Brett looked up at Murphy, a silent thank you mouthed to him. When Guenivere could finally control herself, she looked around, taking the handkerchief that Murphy was holding out for her, frowning at it.

"Cloth? I didn't think anyone used cloth handkerchiefs anymore."

Murphy grinned, glad for a moment to lighten the mood. "You'll find they are still in use. In fact, all my friends carry them. We did before we married. A friend, in fact the police chief of our town, told us we had to, that ladies in distress needed the real thing, not paper. That came from his wife."

"Thank him for me." She rose, her father's arm still around her. "Can I see him? Please? I need to see him."

"That's why I'm here. That's why your father is here. We'll take you to him, but we need to take you on your own. Your father will follow with some of my friends."

She's frowned at him. "Just how many of there are you?"

"Today? Let's see. There's the eight of our team. Abe's brother-in-law tagged along as did a detective friend of ours and also a paramedic friend. I can assure you, we were well prepared for what we would find. And before you ask, we all had what we term now as "adventures"."

She stared at him, not sure he was telling her the truth. At his nod, she simply shook her head and then walked towards the door, stopping as he laid a hand on her arm.

"Just some rules to follow, Guenivere. Just for now. One of us goes through the door first. That's a given. No argument, please. If you argue, you don't go anywhere. I know you trust the men here, but there is someone out there after you. Your friends are working on that. Soon, you'll be free to walk around without an escort. But for now, the word we have received and that Barnabas has received is that you are a target to get to your father. Think of that."

Guenivere had paled as he talked, knowing he was right. She nodded, unable to say a word.

Murphy watched the emotions playing across her face. Thanks, Abe, you had to volunteer me, now didn't you? His hand on her arm led her to the loading dock, where a black SUV waited with the doors open, a second one towards which her father headed. She paused, watching as he was greeted and then tucked inside.

His hand nudging her forward, Murphy tucked her inside the first SUV and then sat beside her, the door closing with an almost silent bang. She frowned at that, leaning around him to gaze at the door.

"Surprised?" Murphy grinned at her nod. "Not what you expected. We made some modifications that we needed to."

"Maybe you could work with Dad on his trucks. Some of those doors really sound loud. But then, the men are always in a hurry." She looked around, taking in the other three men with her, before she turned to the man sitting beside her.

"You're Joseph."

"That would be me. How's your security system?"

"So far, I have no idea. I haven't been working at the office. I'm not allowed." She sat back, sounding disgruntled but a glint of mischief peeked from her eyes. "Who's in front?"

"Ian is our driver. That's Micah in the front passenger seat. Abe, Nathaniel, Luke and Matt are with your Dad. We have Gideon, Frankie and Dave with Branigan."

"I'm still impressed. But where are your ladies? I know you are all married. Didn't you bring them for cover?'

The men shot her a quick glance before breaking out into laughter, which had been her aim.

Chapter 36

Waiting almost impatiently in the SUV where Ian had pulled to a stop near the back of the hospital parking lot, Guenivere peered through the darkened windows, her gaze steadfast on the door of the building, knowing Branigan was there, that he was alive, that God had brought him back to her. She knew why she had to wait, She just didn't know because of who. But then, again, maybe she did.

She looked around at the men, trying to think of a way to ask what she had to. Ian had been watching her closely and his eyes raised to meet Micah's, who nodded.

"Guenivere?" Ian's voice, though low, caused Guenivere to jump as she looked up at him, her hands twisting against one another. "Who do you suspect? Is it someone close to you?"

She hesitated before she nodded. "I haven't been honest with Barnabas. I've given him some names. One of them is a woman on the board." She frowned. "And there's her brother and his wife. I think they are all involved in crime." She blinked rapidly, taking the handkerchief Joseph handed her with a quiet word of thanks. "I never told Dad about how I was physically assaulted when I was young. I meant to but they weren't home when I got there and when the morning came, I was too scared and too ashamed to. She was there. I had driven that memory too deep to bring up.

I wanted to forget." She looked up once more, a woebegone look on her face. "It's my fault, isn't it? My fault that Dad has had to deal with this. That Branigan was kidnapped and then hurt."

"Not at all. You didn't make them do what they did. You did not make them live a life of crime and hide it." Micah's voice was stern. "They made those decisions, not you."

She nodded, not quite convinced that he was correct. She watched as Ian started up the vehicle and pulled closer to the back door, waiting until her father and three of the men with him had entered. Murphy's hand rested on her forearm.

"Just to go back over some things. I know you understand that we are here to protect you. Let us do that. Trust us, please, Guenivere." He watched as she nodded, her eyes fastened on him. "You and I go in through another door from what your father did. Joseph and Micah will follow in a moment. We need to get you in and to the room your police chief has arranged for you. He tells me he was overrun with volunteers to make it safe."

Guenivere nodded, a sober look on her face. "Branigan is an auxiliary officer. They have tried so hard to find him. I just don't understand how you did."

"Abe's wife, Emma, came across an address that seemed to fit but she wasn't sure if it would. Abe talked to your police chief and volunteered us to go in and bring Branigan out if it was true." He watched as her mouth opened and then closed. "It's what we do, Guenivere. It's our livelihood but also our mission."

She nodded once more, a desperate look on her face. "Please? Can I see him?"

"Sure. Just let us do all the looking around. You just stay focused on that door and getting through it." Murphy listened for a moment to Abe's voice through his earpiece before he nodded at the other three. "We're good to go."

Murphy was out of the vehicle, Guenivere's hand in his as he rapidly led her the few feet to the door, opening it quickly and pulling her through. They had researched the hospital with Will's help, trying to judge the best and fastest way to get her in and to the room the hospital had set aside for the family.

A whisper of sound came to Murphy's ear and as he spun towards it, a hard object landing on his head sent him to the ground, Guenivere's scream sounding in his ears before it faded. Guenivere stared down at him and then at the two men in front of her, panic beginning to set in. She backed away, her hand coming up to run along the wall behind her back, trying to reach the door she knew was behind her.

A grubby hand with broken nails grasped her wrist and stopped her in her tracks before she was pulled towards the man, struggling to escape to no avail. She heard the heated words between them, one blaming the other for Murphy being there and then blaming each other because they had to take him out, as they put it.

She pulled with her arm, twisting and turning to break the hard grasp to no avail. She began to flail at her captor, her hand catching at his face, causing him to turn on her in anger, a hand raised that smacked at her face, driving her into the wall and then limply to the floor, the only thing holding her from collapsing totally the hold he had on her.

"Now, what did you do that for?" The second man began to curse in violent terms.

"I had to. You saw her." The first man wiped at his face, his hand finding the blood where Guenivere's nails had caught at the flesh. "She scratched me."

"So. Stop being a baby. We need to get out of here." He turned, ready to pick Guenivere up when he saw the men standing there, grim looks on their faces.

The first man dropped her wrist, starting to back away before he realized his exit was blocked. Their hands raised, the men were herded away by the responding officers and then the door closed behind them.

Micah was on his knees beside Guenivere as Ian dropped beside Murphy.

"Murphy?" He heard a groan from his friend who was sprawled face down. A hand reached for the back of his head.

"Ian? What did I do that I don't remember going and doing?" Murphy slowly raised himself to a sitting position, his hand still cupping the back of his head.

"You got clobbered, is what. But it seems as if Guenivere put up a fight." His head turned towards Micah. "Micah? How is she?"

Micah shook his head, as he stood, then bent to pick her up. "She's out cold, Ian. It looks as if she was slammed into the wall."

Will spoke from behind Ian. "Let's get them to that room. Doc's around. I'll have him come take a look. We have many hands on deck to help."

He stood for a moment, watching as the men walked away, before he turned to Barnabas and Abe.

"I don't like this. They shouldn't have known where they were."

"Those are my thoughts." Abe pondered for a moment. "Guenivere. Her shoes? Purse? Phone? Any jewelry?"

"The only jewelry is the ring Branigan gave her. Her shoes? That's possible. We've been wracking our brains trying to figure out how they knew where she was. She is on, I think, her third or fourth phone in the last few weeks. Branigan has gone over it thoroughly and locked it down as much as he can. He won't even let her have her location app working."

"Good. Now, her purse?"

"She doesn't carry one. She has a folder she sticks what she needs in and that goes into her pocket. Her keys? We've looked them over as well."

"That leaves her shoes, maybe? They may have been watching but someone knew where we were heading and which door we would go in." Abe turned at a sound from Will, whose face was sober.

"I think I know how. The Langs have a young relative, who is close to one of my officers. He was warned not to say anything and to be very careful. It seems that I need to have a chat with him. Care to join me? You can listen in from behind the mirror.”

"Gladly, Will. I want whoever it is that did this. Guenivere did not deserve to be hurt again.” Barnabas walked away, his anger palpable.

Chapter 37

Her head twisting as she roused, Guenivere's hand sought her face, wondering why it felt so cold. Her hand found her face, or so she thought. It's cold. I don't understand why. She twisted at her hand to free it from the one holding it but couldn't.

Lena stood, her hand on her daughter's, watching as Guenivere turned her head in a restless manner, trying to escape the ice pack the nurse had placed against her face. The nurse had simply shook her head at Lena and whispered that if she could, would she make sure it stayed in place as much as it could?

Barnabas had been in and out, worried about Guenivere. He hadn't said much, but Brett had stopped him at one point, a question on his face.

"Barnabas, what news is there?"

The younger man had shrugged, his eyes on his friend's face. Brett had become close to him, becoming almost a mentor to him in some ways.

"I haven't been told much. Will and Dallas are working on an angle. Emma is shooting them as much information as they can get. Our guys are working their hardest, taking a leave from their work to do so. They want this over for Branigan. It has angered them that he disappeared from his home and it has angered them that Guenivere was tracked down at the hospital and then injured."

Brett ran his hands through his hair before dropping them to his side and clenching them. "That angers me too. She's my little girl, Barnabas, always will be. We couldn't have any more. She's our life. I want to see her and Branigan build their own life." He held up a hand as Barnabas opened his mouth. "He came to me one day, just asking in general he said. Would I object if he dated Guenivere? He was honest. Told me he had never dated, had had no desire to. Not until Guenivere."

"We're all like that, Brett. Every single one of the guys at the building. We are waiting on God. I have no idea why the six have gone through what they have, but God does. He has allowed it and it always works out for the couple. Whatever it has been that they have needed to work on, that is how He has dealt with them." He had turned and walked away at that point, leaving Brett to stare after him.

Breck spoke from beside Brett, watching him closely. "He's right, you now. None of us want to put our ladies in danger, but that seems to be the way it is."

Brett turned. "Your ladies? Breck, you're not dating. So why would you say that?"

Breck shrugged, a distant look flickering across his face. "When you're a teenager, you think you know how your life will go, who you'll go out with, who you'll date, who you'll marry. You plan out your life, your work, where you'll live. It doesn't always work out that way." He turned and walked away, a slump to his shoulders that Brett had not seen before.

Lena's arm came around him. "What's with Breck? He looks disheartened."

"He is. I think he had someone in his past and for some reason, they parted ways." He looked down at his wife before dropping a kiss on her forehead. "How's our girl?"

"She's sleeping again, but it's so restless. Doc was by when you were down at the office. He doesn't want to give her too much medication. He says he wants to see how she is. Until she rouses completely, they won't know." She turned him back into the hospital room. "Abe's men are angry."

"Yes, they are. So are the building guys. Buckley said he'd be back around."

Barnabas had found his way down the hall to where Branigan was, hesitating to pray before he entered the room. He searched the hall, a frown on his face, feeling someone watching him. His eye caught the husband of a board member, and he frowned. He should not be here. As far as Barnabas knew, they didn't have any friends or family on this floor.

Instead of pushing the door open, he walked away, his phone out.

"Dallas? Where are you?"

"Barnabas? Just heading for the elevator there. Why?"

"Because Evan Lang is here. He shouldn't be. They don't have anyone on this floor." Barnabas turned to watch, seeing Evan Lang moving towards Branigan's room. "What is he doing? He's heading for Branigan. He shouldn't be. There are no visitors allowed."   His phone was in his pocket and he was rapidly striding towards the door, to stop in front of it, a hand held up to stop Lang.

"What is the meaning of this, Carey? I want to see that man. I think he knows something."

"Right at the moment, he is under police guard. No one not on the authorized list gets in there." Barnabas' face was sober, not reflecting the emotions and thoughts flowing through his mind. He caught Dallas moving quickly towards him, a hand on his weapon, a police officer approaching from the other way. "Sorry."

"Step aside, Carey. I will see him."

Barnabas continued to shake his head. "As his next of kin, no, I won't allow it. The physicians have restricted his visitors. Besides, as I said, he is under police guard."

"I don't see any officer." Lang's arrogance was foremost, and Barnabas wondered how they had ever chosen his wife for the Board.

"There's one in the room. Dallas, the detective on the case, is beside you and another officer is to your left."

"Not hardly likely." Lang's hand came up to shove Barnabas to one side, only he never got a chance. His wrist was grasped and quickly twisted behind him, the click of handcuffs sounding loud in the suddenly quiet corridor. "What is the meaning of this? Take this off. I will have your job, you do know that."

Dallas merely shook his head, reading Lang his rights, before he spoke. "Barnabas is correct. You have attempted to breach police protective custody. Besides, we have a laundry list of questions we need to ask you. The first being: Where is your wife?"

"My wife? Either at work or at home. Why?"

"Because we need to speak with her, and no, she is not at home. Nor is she at work. She hasn't been in either place for a day or so, I'm told." Dallas nodded to the officer, who moved off, hand to Lang's arm, who tried to hurry away from them all, knowing the staff and visitors to the floor were watching.

"He'll try to get your badge, you know." Barnabas broke into a grim smile.

"He can try. We have too much on him. Not directly related to you or the Foundation or even to Branigan. I just wish I knew where his wife is."

Barnabas looked behind him, seeing Abe approaching. "Talk to Abe. By the way he coming at us, I would say he has something important." Barnabas disappeared into Branigan's room, leaving Dallas to turn and face Abe.

"Abe, is it?"

Abe grinned. "It is. Listen. This address? That's where we found Branigan. I talked to Will last night and we went in early this morning. You may find your missing piece of the puzzle there."

Dallas stared at him, before he looked down at the piece Abe had thrust at him. "This place? Patrols have been by there, but didn't see anything that alerted them."

"No, there wouldn't have been. The lane is well travelled. Branigan was in a room in the basement." Abe had to stop, to swallow the anger rising in him. "He was shackled, Dallas, shackled to the wall, only able to move a certain number of feet."

"What?" Dallas was shocked. "Well then, I guess I'm on my way out there." He nodded towards the door. "Doc says he's still out, that he's been mistreated. I have an officer inside and more around the floor. I know you and your team were planning on staying for a day or so."

"We were, but we've been asked to go in and retrieve someone else. We have to leave this afternoon. In fact, I have to run." Abe glanced at his watch, and then headed away from Dallas, his long strides covering the hallway rapidly.

Dallas stared after him and then down at the paper, sighing as he did so. How does she do it, he wondered? How does she find these?

Chapter 38

Stirring early the next morning, Guenivere felt at her face. The pain had lessened but she could feel the swelling. A bruise, she thought. Now how did I do that? Memory flooded to her as her eyes crept open and she glanced around, not moving her head. A hospital room. That's right. I was coming to see Branigan, and someone attacked me. I do hope Murphy is okay, she prayed.

She slid from the bed, waiting for the dizziness she expected, and surprised when it didn't hit. She searched for her clothes, finding them and then opening the doors in the room until she found the bathroom. She dressed quickly and looked around for her shoes, not seeing them. Shrugging, she slipped on her socks and then padded for the door.

Guenivere knew Branigan was there, somewhere, and she was determined to find him, if she had to search the entire hospital. She paused outside her door, her eyes narrowed against the light for a moment, before she headed away from her room, spying the officer standing outside one of the room just down from her.

She paused as she neared, finding him watching her, an encouraging smile of his face as he stepped over to push open the door, a hand beckoning her to move forward.

"He's sleeping, Guenivere, but he has been rousing more and more. I sure he'll wake fully when you are there." John, the officer, held the door, watching as she hesitated for a moment before almost running for the bed.

Her eyes on the IV line running down to Branigan's hand, Guenivere stood for a moment, almost afraid to look at him. Her hand reached to cover his, feeling the thinness of it. Branigan stirred for a moment, before his hand moved away and then covered hers, his grasp tight. She raised her eyes to his face, a sob in her throat, as she saw how thin and white it was. Dark shadows lay heavy under his eyes. Her free hand rested against the beard he had grown, feeling the fever that raged in his body.

Branigan's eyes flickered as he sensed someone near him. Not his guard, he thought. Nor Yvette Lang. He glanced around, frowning. He was free? How, he wondered. And a hospital room. Good. God, You were there. You did rescue me. Thank you. But Guenivere. I don't know where she is. I am so afraid for her. He paused in his prayer, feeling lips touching his forehead gently and then his beloved's voice whispering in his ear that she loved him and would he please wake up all the way. She needed that.

Too tired to comply, Branigan's eyes dropped down and he slept, this time a natural healing sleep. Guenivere brushed at the tears of her face, tears of thankfulness, joy, but also worry. He hadn't roused enough, she thought. Fatigue hit her in giant waves, to the point her eyelids felt weighted down. She finally gave in and just crawled up beside him, moving his arm so she could snuggle close. She really didn't care if the staff would complain. Branigan was back to her, and that was all she cared about.

The nurse who entered, paused, and then just shook her head. There is no harm, she thought. I would be doing the same. She moved quietly around the room before the door opened and Doc entered.

Doc stood for a moment, before he looked over at Susan, the nurse, and just smiled.

"How is he?"

"Vitals are getting better. His fever is still there, but it seems to be reducing." She nodded at Guenivere. "I was looking for her and then John at the door told me she was in here."

"And so she is. They've had a rough few weeks, Susan. And until they round up everyone, they are still not safe."

"How close are they?"

Doc shrugged. "I have no idea. Will or Dallas haven't said much to Barnabas or Brett but I'm sure they're working hard to find everyone."

"What was that I heard about Yvette Lang?"

"And that would be?"

"I heard they found her dead, at the bottom of the stairs in her parents' old house."

"That may be. I haven't heard that confirmed."

"If it is true, then I'm glad. She has been nothing but trouble to any of us here or even in town."

Doc frowned at Susan's words. "What do you mean?"

"I mean that she has tried to interfere in anyone's treatment that she has been related to. She has come on the floors and tried to rearrange staffing and how we do things."

"She has? Obviously it didn't work."

"No, it didn't. The hospital director finally had to put her in her place and ban her from here for a while."

Doc nodded, his eyes going to Branigan as he stirred. "Then, if it's true, that is one less thing you will all have to worry about. Now, Branigan is awakening. Let's see how he is. Paul asked me to cover for him for a while. He had a family emergency he had to attend to."

Chapter 39

Hearing his name called, thinking the voice sounded familiar, Branigan struggled to open his eyes, finally succeeding, a hand coming up to block the low level of the light in the room. He looked around, finding Doc standing beside him, a hand on his wrist.

"Branigan? You're awake? How are you feeling?"

Branigan swallowed hard, moving his lips, before he could speak, his voice rough and hoarse. "Okay, I think. I'm in a hospital?"

"You are. You're safe." Doc watched the relief that flowed his face. "You're dehydrated, malnourished, and running a fever. You'll be here for a few days."

Branigan nodded, not wanting to ask the obvious, unsure as to why Doc stood there, a grin on his face. He coughed, before he felt a heaviness on his shoulder. "What did I do to the shoulder, Doc?"

"Nothing." Doc continued to grin, not explaining.

Branigan's head twisted, his chin brushing against soft hair, before he stilled, his head raising slightly to stare down at the body he had tight in his arm.

"Guenivere?"

"It is. She was hurt coming in to find you, but now it seems as if her world's all right again. Susan found her here a while ago."

"She just had to do this, didn't she?" Branigan's comment was soft, his face lighting with the love he felt for his lady. "Doc, when can we do a wedding?"

"A wedding, is it?" Doc looked up as he heard a choked sound from Susan, catching the merriment on her face.

"Yes. I had time to think when I was held captive. Too much time. I don't want to wait any longer than I have to. She means too much to me. I want whatever time God has decided we get."

Doc had been watching Guenivere, seeing when her eyes had opened and she had looked up at Branigan, her body staying still.

"I see. I guess you'll be needing then to speak with Brett and Lena and then Buckley."

"We have plans, Branigan, Mom and I. Buckley knows. They all do. He's just waiting for us to give him a date." Guenivere's voice was soft, soft enough that Branigan had trouble following her words.

"We do? You have been busy, my love."

"They know, Branigan. They guessed it the day or so after you were taken. Cadee told me I should be wearing your ring. That you would want me to."

Branigan rested his cheek against her hair, knowing that Doc and Susan had stepped outside, leaving them alone. "I do. We had plans for that night, plans that God saw fit to set aside."

"He did. Now, we need to get you better. Buckley will be around, I have no doubt of that."

He nodded, a frown forming. "It wasn't our guys that came in, was it? We have done things like that before. We went in and found Baird and brought he and Berneen out."

"No. Abe Finlay appeared with his men and three of his friends, I think he said. He talked to Will about an address his wife had found."

"Okay. So it was them. I really didn't know for sure."

She waited for him to continue, but he slept, a deep, dreamless sleep, one that he needed so desperately. Guenivere finally sat up, her eyes on his face before she reached to kiss him and then slipped away from him, heading for the waiting room, knowing she would find friends and likely family there.

Lena stood as her daughter appeared, wrapping her in her arms, tears she could not control on her face. Guenivere leaned back, then hugged her mother tighter.

"I'm okay, Mom. I really am. And so in Branigan. We need to talk about what he went through, but he's been awake." She was aware of movement around her. She looked up, not surprised to see the thirteen friends and the ladies there. "He's going to be okay. Doc said so."

“And if Doc said so, then it must be true.” Buckley reached to hug her, a prayer audible in the silence.

“Buckley? Branigan wants to set a day.” She laughed, a sudden happy carefree laugh, one they had not heard from her before, and one her mother had not heard in years. “He was awake enough that that was what he asked for.”

“That we can do. You just tell me when. We will make it work.”

Chapter 40

Two weeks later, Branigan dropped down into the chair behind the desk in his office. He was back to work, only part time, but he needed to be, both for his mental health and also for his clients. He flipped through the pile of papers on his desk, and then reached for his office schedule. It was clear for now, but that was usually how it worked. He would take calls, make his appointments, then his assessments, and wait for the client to either accept his recommendations or refuse them.

Deep into his work, multiple phone calls returned, Branigan lifted his head, thinking he had heard the door to the reception area open and close. He shook his head. No, he thought, I locked it. There can't be anyone out there. His concentration went back to his work, before he raised his head again. This time, he knew he had heard a key in the door and the door open. Not many people had keys, Guenivere one of them. He glanced at his watch. That must be her.

"Guenivere? Is that you?" He listened, not hearing anything. He did not like that she didn't respond. Hands on his chair arms, he shoved back, ready to rise, freezing in place as he saw Guenivere appear in his doorway, a hand around her mouth, a gun to her temple. His eyes narrowed in fear as he watched her stop just inside the office. She was angry, he could tell, and he couldn't say that he blamed her, not one bit.

"On your feet, Clery. We're going to go on a little trip."

Branigan stayed where he was, his eyes on Guenivere's, a slight frown marring his forehead. She is up to something, but what? He shook his head.

"Sorry, Langton. Not happening." Branigan rested his arms on the desk top. "We're not going anywhere."

"She dies, if you don't." The gun wavered, Guenivere cringing away from it, not sure if she would survive.

"No, I don't think so." Branigan had heard the door once more, quiet on its opening, and then saw Dallas appear in the background. "Somehow, I don't think so."

Dallas moved forward, his hand on his own weapon, and reached around to grasp the man's wrist, jerking it upright as it fired. Guenivere had dropped to the ground, curling up in a ball, her arms over her head, as far away from the men as they struggled as she could get.

Dallas finally shoved Langton towards the officer. "Take him away. He's one we've been looking for." He turned, ready to help Guenivere, finding Branigan had made it to her first. He had not seen Branigan clear the top of his desk as he raced to his sweetheart.

"Guenivere?" He was on the floor, cradling her to him, his arms tight around her. "Are you okay?"

"I am. Just as mad as a hornet, as my Grandmother used to say. How did he get in? The door was locked."

"It was?" Dallas crouched down in front of her. "We'll search him, but he either had a key or picked the lock." He looked up at a sound from Branigan. "Branigan?"

"Look at the newest hire in our security team. He looks like him, but the names are different. I am sure he had a thorough background check, but something is off."

"Something is definitely off. I'll be in touch. Now, can you two please stay out of trouble?" With a wave, he was gone.

Branigan just sat, holding Guenivere, who made no move away from him, content to be held in his arms.

She finally turned, her face close to his. "Branigan, what are we to do? Is he the last?"

"I suspect so. I talked to Dallas earlier. He indicated he had one more person to track down. That would be Langton, I suspect. He'll need some time to wrap it all up, but then he'll tell us all about it." He kissed her, lingering for a moment, before he leaned back. "Now, about that date."

"What date? Are you asking me out on a date? I accept. High heels. Dress. Makeup. Jewelry. The whole night yards." She tapped at her chin. "Oh, yes. Tuxedo for you."

Branigan stared at her, open mouthed until her finger tapped under his chin. He swallowed hard.

"Yeah, sure. If that's what you want." When she didn't reply, his eyes narrowed. He finally caught the gleam of mischief on her face, earning her another long kiss.

"No, it's okay, Branigan. I know what you're asking." She giggled, suddenly free of the past, of the lost hope, of the lost time she felt she had wasted. "God has restored hope to me, in so many ways. You have been a huge part of how He has worked."

"For both of us, sweetheart. For both of us. Now, about that date?"

Her head on his shoulder, she finally nodded. "I know. We need to set one. Everybody keeps asking." She raised her head to stare at him, wondering at the laughter shaking his body. "What did I say?"

"It's not what you said. It's what happened with Brady and Fynn. Buckley made the mistake of telling Fynn he had a Saturday open, would it do for their wedding. Brady shot his words right back at him, taking him up on his offer."

Guenivere went off in peals of laughter. "That's what he meant, then. He told me he had Saturday free, would it do?"

Branigan shook with deeper laughter. He rose, his hand out to help Guenivere to her feet. "Well, then, we'll track him down and ask if it will do. I don't want to rush you."

"You're not. Mom and I have the plans made. I have my dress, hers actually. You need to arrange for the license or rather we do. You get the flowers. Anna has said the ladies at the church want to do the meal for us, with the ladies here helping." She stopped, her hand over her mouth in shock, causing Branigan to duck his head to stare at her and ask what now. "Who do I choose as my attendant? The five ladies are all so precious to me."

"Then, have them all. They'd be happy to. If it's okay with you, I would like a nice simple ceremony. Not too fancy. You're the main part for me."

"Then, I'm glad you said that. That's what Mom and I want. I sure the ladies would have a dress they could wear without any expense."

Branigan paused for a moment. "You do realize that when we marry, you become an employee of the Foundation as well? That you receive a salary from it?"

She nodded. "I do. That's part of my hesitation, I think. Dad has paid me well. I just don't know if I feel comfortable taking one."

Chapter 41

That Saturday, Branigan and Guenivere mingled with their friends, glad to be able to do so without any shadow hanging over them. Dallas had been by the day before, having asked to meet with them.

When he left, they had just stared at one another, and then at Brett and Lena, who both sat at their kitchen table, shock on their faces.

"I never knew." Brett had trouble understanding that his cousin, Donald, had been behind part of what had happened. That he had made plans to take over Brett's trucking company and use it for smuggling and evil. Brett had not asked what all the plans were, but from the look on Dallas' face, he decided that he didn't want to know.

"You had no idea, Dad?" Guenivere turned to her father, her hands rolling her mug.

"None at all, or I would have ended it long before this." He looked over at Lena. "You said something years ago but we just let it go."

"I did. I wondered if he was involved in crime, but he covered it too well for me to be certain."

Branigan had been listened to their conversation, before he spoke. "Donald? Is he the one from the central part of the province? Then, Emma picked up on that. She couldn't confirm anything, which is unusual for her."

"It is, but he hid it behind companies and people. There was never a record of him being involved, until the Langs were arrested. Yvette played us, and we feel the fools for that. But justice has been served for her. God looked after that."

"She wasn't well, Dad. I could see it in her face." Guenivere paused, not sure how to continue. "It was hard, what we went through." Her eyes turned to her betrothed and she reached for his hand. "But God was there, every step of the way. He kept us alive. He restored our hope, hope that I never thought would ever return. So, in a way, I am glad."

Lena finally spoke after they had spent time in prayer. "I know, Guenivere, that you have struggled for years. You just wouldn't tell us. But now that the Langs and Langton are charged, we can move on. Your Dad has said he wants to retire. Douglas is willing to buy into the company and run it on a daily basis. He's finding the mechanics work getting to be hard on him. His son wants to take over that. Your Dad would still be involved, but as a silent partner."

"Dad? Really? That's great. Then, you can work in the mission like you wanted to."

"That's exactly it, Guenivere. With what you went through, we realized that God was calling us to move on, to move forward to something new and exciting."

Branigan's attention came back to the present, as Blair and Brady stopped beside him. He could see his other friends mingling with the church family.

"Branigan? You really are okay?" Blair still held concern for his friend.

"I'm getting there. I've been in counselling, not with Buckley, but with a trusted Christian counsellor. That has helped." He nodded towards Guenivere. "Knowing she's safe? That makes a huge difference."

"You two did have an adventure, not as life threatening as Bradon's, but still life changing." Brady hesitated. "The six of us make a team. Barnabas has asked that we meet on a weekly basis for now, to share with one another how we're doing, to pray for one another. Our ladies have already planned on that."

"They have? I can see that. And yes, I think it's a good idea." His arm swept his bride tight to his side. "We'll plan on that. Dallas has asked that he meet with us all in a couple of weeks, just to finalize what he knows. Trevor Lang had a heart attack last night, he tells me. He is not expected to survive."

"God's avenging once more." Guenivere looked at the two other men. "We can plot our revenge but we have to leave it in God's hands."

Two months later, Guenivere turned from her desk, tidying up the paperwork she had been immersed in. Douglas had asked her to stay on in the office and she had agreed to do that part time. His daughter had asked for some training to work the other hours, and Guenivere had agreed happily. She had become involved in the mission with her parents, looking after the little ones for a few hours a week, and enjoying it immensely.

Branigan stood, shoulder propped against the door, his eyes on her, wonder in his heart that she was his. He shoved away and walked over, dropping a kiss on the upturned mouth, before he perched on her desk.

"Done for the day?"

"I am." She sat back, mischief on her face. "And if I hadn't been?"

"Then I would has asked you to play hooky. I had a picnic basket delivered to my office with strict instructions that you and I were to go on a picnic."

"Mom's at it again."

"Actually, no. It wasn't your Mom. It was Barnabas' mother. She arranged for Anna to deliver it. She told me I had to court you, that we had missed out on a couple of weeks, and needed to make up for that."

"She did? She is so sweet." Guenivere stood, to be enveloped in his arms. "We have a picnic waiting, buster." Her comment came when she could breathe again.

He laughed as he stood, his hand reaching for hers. "That we do, my Proverbs 31 bride. That we do."

She laughed at him, knowing he was flirting with her, but enjoying it.

"Branigan? Where can we volunteer together? You volunteer with the police. I volunteer with the mission. But I would really like to see us work together somewhere."

"That we can do. I heard from a friend today about an animal rescue that is looking for help. They take in strays that have no homes and train them as service dogs."

"Oh! Yes! That sounds like something we could do."

Branigan laughed at her. "Then, I guess I did okay when I arranged for us to go out there Saturday to look around and see if it's a fit."

Her sudden hug stopped him in his tracks. He felt blessed, knowing he had the lady God had planned for him, work he enjoyed, and friends he could share his life with.

Dear Readers

Thank you for picking up the story of Branigan and his Proverbs 31 lady, Guenivere. It was another one of those stories that I was just along for the ride on. I had no idea where they planned to go. In fact, Guenivere was to be a Gemma, until I was emphatically told that no, she was not a Gemma. I was ordered to find another name for her.

Hope. Such a precious thing to have. When we lose hope in life, in whatever, it destroys part of us. God does not want that. He wants us to have the hope of His salvation, and through that, hope in whatever He has for us. So many times over the years, I have been discouraged, lost hope, but God has always brought me through and restored me to walk correctly in His presence.

Never be afraid to tell Him what and how you are feeling. It's what He wishes. When we are honest with Him and ask for forgiveness and restoration, He does just that.

My father referred quite often to Proverbs 31 as a picture of a godly woman. It is so true. When, as ladies, we walk with God, our lives will reflect the characteristics shown in those verses. That's what we strive for, isn't it?

Dear Abe and his team just had to show up. I miss these characters from *His Guardians*. They seem to like to show up when I least expect them to. It is never planned. And in this book, they brought in Gideon from *The Haven* and Frankie from *The Storm*, part of the *Haven of Rest* trilogy and Dave, from *A Touch of His Garment.* All beloved characters.

God bless each one of you. May you rest in His love.

Ronna

www.ingramcontent.com/pod-product-compliance
Lightning Source LLC
Chambersburg PA
CBHW061254210726
48293CB00003B/954